Ruthless Vow

Ruthless
Book 3

Roxy Sloane

Roxy Sloane Books

Copyright © 2022 by AAHM Inc/Roxy Sloane

All rights reserved.

No part of this book may be reproduced in any form or by any electronic or mechanical means, including information storage and retrieval systems, without written permission from the author, except for the use of brief quotations in a book review.

Cover design by British Empire Designs

❦ Created with Vellum

Also by Roxy Sloane:

THE FLAWLESS TRILOGY:
1. Flawless Desire (Caleb & Juliet)
2. Flawless Ruin (Caleb & Juliet)
3. Flawless Prize (Caleb & Juliet)

THE RUTHLESS TRILOGY:
1. Ruthless Heart (Nero & Lily)
2. Ruthless Games (Nero & Lily)
3. Ruthless Vow (Nero & Lily)

THE PRICELESS TRILOGY
1. Priceless Kiss (Sebastian & Avery)
2. Priceless Secret (Sebastian & Avery)
3. Priceless Fate (Sebastian & Avery)

THE TEMPTATION DUET:
1. One Temptation
2. Two Rules

THE KINGPIN DUET:
1. Kingpin
2. His Queen

Explicit: A Standalone Novel

Also by Roxy Sloane...

THE SEDUCTION SERIES:

1. The Seduction
2. The Bargain
3. The Invitation
4. The Release
5. The Submission
6. The Secret
7. The Exposé
8. The Reveal

Ruthless : Book Three

Ruthless Vow

I made a deal with the devil.

Mafia prince, Nero Barretti. The boy I once loved... And now the man who controls my fate.

I thought I knew the price I was paying, but he won't stop until I belong to him.

Forever.

THE RUTHLESS TRILOGY:

1. Ruthless Heart
2. Ruthless Games
3. Ruthless Vow

Chapter 1

Lily

There's a dull ringing in my ears. Heat. The roar of a fire blazing. A sharp pain blossoming in the back of my skull.

What the hell just happened?

I roll over on the hard asphalt, groaning out loud. My breath has been knocked from my lungs, and when I press my palms to the ground, I feel the slice of broken glass digging into my skin.

Breathe. Think. Get the hell up!

My head is spinning, and I feel dizzy, but I pull myself into a seated position and look around. The wreckage of a car is blazing nearby, half the bodywork scattered around, smoking and smashed like rubble.

I squint at it, ears still ringing, and slowly, the fragments of the last ten minutes come drifting back to me.

I'm at the docks. I came here to warn Nero, about... Something.

I frown, still foggy, grabbing at strands of information.

He was meeting someone, with one of his mafia lieutenants... Vance...

The mole. He was here to find out who was ratting the Barretti organization to the FBI. But he had the wrong guy.

I get a flash of Vance clicking a ballpoint pen. The pen from the hotel where the FBI liked to meet.

It's Vance.

The mole is Vance. That's what I came here to warn Nero about!

I clamber to my feet and look around. "Nero?" I call, my voice scratchy from the smoke. "Nero!"

There's smoke everywhere, flames billowing from the wreckage of the car. I can't see him anywhere.

The car. Nero's car.

I stop dead, the last pieces of my memory slotting into place. Watching as Vance snuck away and fixed a device to Nero's car... Wondering if I should warn my husband—or let him burn... The war between my head and heart raging, until I finally lurched from my hiding place and raced to save him.

But I was too late.

"NERO!" I scream into the darkness, desperate.

But there's no reply. Vance is long gone. I'm alone on the docks. I watch the fireball blaze, an inferno in the dark, and feel my heart rip in two.

Is the man I love dead?

I fight my way closer, shielding my face from the flames. The explosion has left metal and rubber burning in a hollowed-out shell, and fear stabs ice-cold in my chest as I scan the wreckage, looking for my husband.

There!

I spot a figure on the ground, thrown clear of the blast beside some trash cans. He's facedown, and I rush over, kneeling at his side and heaving him over onto his back.

"Nero," I plead, my voice thick with emotion. "Nero, wake up. *Please.*"

His eyes are shut, unmoving. There's cuts and blood on his face. He's not breathing.

Oh God, he's not breathing.

I have no idea what I'm doing as I bring my hands together at the center of his chest and start compressions. I've never done anything like this before, but I have to try, tears stinging in my eyes as I desperately try to bring him back.

"You can't die on me!" I yell at his lifeless body, out of my mind. "You can't. Not when you made me love you, you bastard."

I don't count. I have no idea how many times I'm supposed to do this, anyway. I just stop when it feels right, pinching his nose and blowing into his mouth the way I've seen in TV shows and movies.

Time seems to stop as I continue my attempt at CPR, screaming out for help when I'm doing the compressions. Why hasn't anyone come yet? Why am I left here trying to save the life of the man I've hated half my life?

Why do I need him to live, when for so long, I've wished him dead?

Because I love him.

I've loved him ever since I knew what it was to love someone. And every good memory I have, has him in it. I can see them all now, a heartwrenching movie of our history, from the moment this cocky boy smiled at me for the first time, back when we were just teenagers, to the last time I kissed him and held him close, grown adults bound together by choice and fate.

He's the only one for me. But is this the last time I'll ever hold him?

I don't have the answers, just the rhythmic, desperate pace of my chest compressions, and the sound of my sobs in the dark.

Finally, after what feels like an eternity, Nero's eyes snap open and he gasps for air, coughing.

Oh, thank you God.

Relief washes over me, and I sag back, shaking. "It's OK," I manage to tell him. "You're going to be OK."

Nero turns to his side and wheezes, recovering. The fire is still burning wildly behind us, but I don't care about that. Nothing matters except the fact that Nero's alive.

Barely.

When he finally stops coughing and collapses back onto his back, I cradle his head in my lap.

"Talk to me," I urge him, trying to find the source of all his bleeding. "Nero, can you hear me?"

He groans in pain, mumbling, his breath still shallow. My hands are sticky with blood now, it's coming from a wound in the back of his head. *Fuck.*

"Lily?"

I hear my name being yelled, and then the sound of running footsteps pounds closer. I look up. It's Kyle, one of Nero's drivers, and I've never been so happy to see a familiar face.

"It was some kind of bomb," I babble, "His car, it exploded. He was right beside it. He wasn't breathing."

Kyle takes in the sight of Nero, bleeding on the ground.

"We've got to get him out of here," he says grimly. "Help me get him to the car. Now!"

Together, we haul Nero up, and half-carry, half-drag him to where Kyle parked the car. It's not easy since Nero is a beast of a man and barely hanging on to consciousness, but Kyle is stronger than he looks, and I'm still running on pure fear and adrenaline. I don't know how Kyle knew we were here, but I don't care. I just focus on helping support as much of Nero's weight between us as I can until we can lay him out in the backseat, his head cradled in my lap.

"We have to get him to the hospital," I say, running my eyes over Nero's body, looking for more signs of injuries. But it's too hard to tell how badly he's hurt in the car's dark interior. "He's bleeding, he hit his head. There could be all kind of internal injuries."

"No..." Nero murmurs, his eyes still closed. "No hospital."

"Ignore him," I command Kyle. "Let's go. Lenox Hill is closest. Now!"

But Kyle pauses. "You heard him. No hospitals."

"Are you crazy? He could die!" I sound as hysterical as I feel.

Kyle guns the engine, and I think I've gotten through to him... Until we speed through traffic, and I realize that he's taking us home, to the house in the West Village. "Wait. No," I start, but Kyle meets my eyes in the rearview mirror.

"He's still the boss," he tells me, looking stubborn. We pull up at the house, where there's already people waiting at the curb: Nero's second-in-command, Chase, and an older guy, in his fifties maybe, looking rumpled like he was just pulled out of bed.

Which, knowing the Barretti organization, he probably was. At gunpoint.

"You the doctor?" Kyle demands, getting out.

He nods. "Get him inside. Keep him steady. And you," he says, eyes landing on me. "Tell me exactly what happened. Everything. Go."

I trail them inside, dazed as I recount everything I remember doing once I found him. Chase and Kyle carry Nero into the back of the house, and lay him out on the couch in the den. I watch in horror as the doctor strips his clothing off, revealing purple bruises and more dark, sticky blood.

"Blood bags, in my case," he snaps, not looking up.

I hesitate, reeling.

"Christ, will someone get me the blood?" he roars. "I won't have enough. His pulse is too weak. What's your blood type?"

There's silence.

"You! What's his blood type?"

I realize he's yelling at me. "I... I... I don't know," I blurt, feeling terrible. I'm his wife. I'm supposed to know.

"Then we'll need a universal donor," the doctor says. "O-negative."

"I have it," Kyle speaks up.

"Good, get over here." The doctor beckons. Kyle rolls up his sleeve, the doctor producing ugly looking needles and plastic tubing. He sticks Kyle, who barely winces, and the tubing starts to fill with blood as the doctor preps Nero's arm, too.

"Wait, is that safe?" I blurt, watching them, panicked. This is all wrong. We should be at a hospital, with real doctors, and an operating room. "What are you doing?"

They ignore me.

"Listen to me!" I cry, losing it. "Stop, stop this!"

"Someone get her out of here," the doctor demands, not looking up. Chase roughly grabs me and hustles me out of the room.

"No!" I fight, trying to stay. "I'm not leaving him!"

Chase scowls. "You've done enough, Princess."

He shoves me into the hallway and slams the door in my face.

I stumble back, sinking against the wall, and sliding to the ground. Exhaustion hits me, and it's all I can do to gulp in panicked lungfuls of air. They'll save him, won't they?

They have to save him.

. . .

I don't know how long I sit there, collapsed on the floor. I'm dimly aware of Chase and Kyle coming and going from the room, carrying towels, water, bloodstained clothing. But I'm spent. I can't stop thinking about the moment the car bomb went off. I'd never been so scared in my life. The sound seems to echo in my ears even now.

"Lily!"

I blink and realize that Miles is standing in front of me, and the look on his face makes me think he's been trying to get my attention for a while. How long have I been sitting here, reliving what happened to Nero?

I slowly get to my feet. My mind feels sluggish, and I take a deep breath, trying to shake off this feeling of shock and dread.

The door to the den is still shut. What does that mean?

"... Lily?"

I blink. "I-I'm sorry. What?" I ask.

"Here," Miles leads me gently down the hall, away from whatever the doctor is doing with Nero's broken body. "You're still in shock."

In the kitchen, I find a crowd has gathered. Avery, Chase, and some of Nero's other inner circle. They're milling around, the mood grim. The minute I walk in, there's a barrage of questions.

"How is he?"

"What the hell happened tonight?"

"I-I don't..." I swallow hard. "I don't know."

"He had a meeting at the docks," Avery speaks up grimly. Her eyes are red, and she looks like she's been crying—not that she'd ever show weakness in front of this crowd. "Something about a lead, to the mole."

"It was an ambush then," Chase announces.

"Fucking Feds," someone mutters.

"Or the Kovacks," Chase agrees. "Either way, whoever's

behind this won't live to see another day, I'll make fucking sure of it."

Vance.

I remember his betrayal and look around. But there's no sign of him. He's probably long gone by now.

"Lily?" Avery studies me. "What is it?"

I hesitate, then shake my head. "Nothing."

I'm not ready to share what I know. And besides, how can I prove it? I only know Vance is connected to the FBI because I was in that hotel meeting them myself. I didn't go through with selling out Nero, but I'm not about to incriminate myself in a room full of his men, ready to go to war with any traitors.

I feel a chill, remembering my precarious position here. I'm Nero's wife—by law, if not by choice. But it's only his protection that's kept me alive so far. He told me himself: Without him, there are plenty of Barretti guys who would happily make me pay for my father's betrayal of the organization, ten years ago.

I need him. Alive.

But as if in response to my fevered prayer, the doctor emerges into the kitchen. I'm taking a sip of water, but when I see the blood on his shirt and the grave expression on his face, I lose my grip.

SMASH.

The glass shatters on the floor, and everyone shuts up, turning to see me. And the doctor.

"No..." I whisper, my voice trembling.

The doctor exhales. "I'm afraid there was nothing I could do," he says, refusing to meet my eyes. "His injuries were too severe."

My legs give way and I grab the counter for balance. "Are you saying..."

I can't even utter the words.

"Nero didn't make it."

The world spins as I hear the shocked reactions around me.

No.

I can't believe it. I can't. I would know. I would *feel* it. Because without him...

Before I know what I'm doing, I lunge for the hallway. "Wait!" the doctor calls, but I ignore him, charging past, straight for the den. I fling open the door, not even thinking about what I might find on the other side.

But whatever I could imagine, it's not this.

Nero's body is sprawled on the couch. He's got bandages and bruises on his naked chest, bloody towels crumpled on the floor. And his eyes... are open.

He raises his head to look at me and offers a weak glare. "Miss me, Princess?"

And I just about stop breathing.

He's alive.

Chapter 2

Lily

He's alive.

Thank God.

I catch my breath, unsteady. Relief crashes over me... only to be followed by confusion – and fury. Nero is alive. The doctor just lied to me.

"What the hell is going on?" I ask, still shaken to my core. Chase comes storming into the den behind me, cursing under his breath.

"I tried to stop her."

"Close the door, Chase," Nero says, then he shifts into a seated position, elevated by some pillows. "And for God's sake, keep your voice down," he tells me.

As if it's *my* fault.

"Are you kidding me?" I fight not to scream the roof down. I'm still trembling, trying not to cry. "I thought you were dead!"

"Yeah, it's an unfortunate necessity that people believe that for a while."

"People?" I spit. "I'm your *wife.*"

"Are you, now?" Nero's eyes meet mine coolly. Then he

shrugs, like my terror is no big deal. "Vance will go to ground now; he won't risk retribution. But we don't know who else is involved in this. It could be anyone. Anyone I trust, even. But if people think I'm dead, it will give me a chance to draw them out." He looks past me to Chase.

"You get the surveillance footage from the docks yet?"

"Working on it."

Nero nods, looking grim. "I doubt there's anything on there. I didn't see anyone aside from Vance. But... Fuck, if Kyle hadn't followed me there, who knows what might have happened?"

His gaze slides past me, and I realize... *He doesn't remember that I was there.*

I consider telling him, but I decide to keep my mouth shut. I don't want him to know just how much I cared, or how scared I was when I thought he was dead.

"Lily, you understand what's at stake here?" he demands. "Not a fucking word."

"Fine," I mutter. "I won't tell anyone you're alive. Just let me out of here."

Nero's eyes shift to Chase, and he gives him a small nod. Obedient as always, Chase steps aside. I glare as I pass him, not even bothering to look back at Nero. I just need to get away from him, from everyone. The past few hours of chaos and panic are catching up with me, and all I want is to be alone.

Luckily, everyone's cleared out, and the house is empty. I head upstairs, my feet weighing heavier with every step. I make it as far as my art studio and take a seat in the chair by the window. I give in to tears, and weep, my shoulders shaking with the release.

It's been a hell of night.

In fact, the last twenty-four hours have been a whirlwind of emotion.

Finally, the tears ebb, and I begin to feel human again. I

swallow hard, looking around at the half-packed case by the door, and all my supplies shoved into boxes. Now that I know Nero is going to be okay, I remember why I was ready to leave him just a few short hours ago. This bullshit about faking his death is just another example of his betrayal and dishonesty.

I can't trust him.

I shiver, sitting there alone in the dark. As much as my heart aches for him, as much as I felt it breaking when I thought he was dead, it doesn't change what I've learned.

The Barrettis killed my mother.

Nero's father may have issued the order, but Nero was right there by his side. It may not have been his finger on the trigger, but her blood is on his hands, all the same.

He's a killer. A criminal.

My *husband*.

I let out a sob. He knew about it when he married me and didn't say a word. What other secrets is he hiding?

What other terrible crimes are lurking in his past?

Coming here, back under the same roof with him, it blinded me to reality. He was my first love, the only man who's ever claimed my heart. And my body. Our sexual connection, the passion, it swept me up into thinking that he's changed. That we could be something real, away from all the mafia complications and our parents' old betrayals. A fresh start.

But even though a part of me may always love him...

Is that love enough?

I sit a little straighter, making a decision. The only one I can: to protect myself. Hardening my heart against him is the only option. The affection that drove me to follow him tonight, to save his life, it has to be the last kindness I show him. Because if I let myself love him again...

I know, it'll be the end of me.

Somebody clears their throat in the doorway, and I startle. It's the doctor.

"I'm sorry to interrupt, Mrs. Barretti—"

I wince. "Lily, please."

He nods. "I'd like to talk to you about your husband's condition."

"Fine." I nod, tired.

"Well, first of all, I don't want you to worry. Nero will make a full recovery."

He pauses, and I know that he's expecting some kind of reaction from me, probably relief. Well, he's not getting that.

"Is that all?" I ask, folding my arms across my chest.

"Uh... N-no. I just wanted to give you a full rundown of his injuries."

I can tell that he's shocked by my cold reaction as he tells me about Nero's scrapes and bruises. He has a couple of bruised ribs and a minor concussion, and he lost a lot of blood. Overall, it's a miracle that he isn't more injured, considering the circumstances.

"I gave him a bottle of pain meds, and you'll want to make sure that he follows the directions. They're strong."

"Anything else?"

"No, I guess not." He gives me another puzzled look. "I'll check back tomorrow. Well, I guess it's tomorrow now, isn't it? Either way, call if anything else comes up."

He pauses, then exits. I hear him head downstairs and talk in a low voice with Chase in the foyer. A moment later, they both leave. The door closes behind them.

I'm alone.

Except, not really. Nero is still down there, planning God knows what.

Curiosity sends me down the stairs again. I find Nero in the kitchen, looking pained as he tries to reach for a glass from the cabinet.

My instinct is to go to him and see what I can do to help, but I force myself to stay where I am.

He looks over. "I need a glass of water," he says.

I stare back. "The faucet's right there."

Hobbling across the room, Nero reaches the sink. He runs the cold water, then pops a couple of those painkillers.

"Thanks a lot for the help," he says, voice thick with sarcasm. "It's nice to know that I've got such a loving wife."

My temper flares. "What do you expect, after everything you've done?"

He meets my eyes in an even stare. "If this is about your mom..."

"For a start, yes," I reply, my blood like ice in my veins. "Are you even sorry they killed her?"

Nero doesn't flinch. "They did what needed to be done. She should have known what would happen, betraying Roman," he adds grimly. "These are the rules of the game."

"Of *your* game."

"*Ours*," he corrects me. "You're a Barretti too, now, and don't you forget it," He gives me frustrated scowl. "Look around, Lily. You seem pretty happy to enjoy the protection of the Barretti name when it suits you. Well, that protection is *earned*. Our name inspires fear and loyalty for a reason. And I'm getting pretty fucking tired of your judgement when that name is the only reason that you're alive right now."

I catch my breath, hating the truth in his words. "For your information, I'm not judging you," I snap back. "I'm observing. You're a killer, Nero. It's a fact." I count them off. "My mom. That guy you beat and left for dead, and now... Well, I doubt that Vance is going to survive whatever you're planning. You're a killer," I repeat, with a cold fury. "How could I ever love a man like that?"

His expression darkens, and he moves closer until he's just inches away. I want to back away, but I'm tired of cowering to him. There's a fierce possession in his eyes that sends a shiver down my spine, despite myself.

"Don't act so innocent, Princess," he drawls, breath hot on my cheek. "You're the same as me."

"No," I vow, shaking my head.

"Yes," he insists, and it's like he's seeing right through me, into the dark of my deepest fears. "You're a survivor, aren't you? Trying your best to clean up your father's past mistakes. You've already proven you'd do whatever it takes to protect your brother. Your family. There's no line you won't cross. No law you won't break."

I gulp, but I can't deny what he's saying. And Nero sees it in my eyes, he knows me better than anything.

"Yeah, I thought so, Princess," he croons, leaning closer. "All my darkness, my violence... There's a reason you can't stay away. It's because you know you're capable of it, too. We're bound together, you and me," he vows. "We always have been. And the sooner you quit lying to yourself and admit it, the better."

For a moment, we're suspended there together in the dim kitchen lights. Then he reaches for me. His mouth is hot, demanding, and I part my lips on instinct, his tongue sliding deep against my own. Heat blooms inside as he yanks me closer, his hands sliding over my body, knowing exactly where to tease and caress as his mouth works its wicked magic.

I need him.

My traitorous body wants to give in to this, to take the pleasure that I know he can give me,. but my mind lingers on everything that's wrong between us. My anger burns hotter than my passion, and I tear myself away, panting.

"No," I manage, reeling back. "You're wrong," I insist. "I'm *nothing* like you!"

I turn to go, Nero's mocking laughter following me to the door. "Tell yourself that if you want.

But we have a meeting tomorrow afternoon, and you better play the part of devoted wife. Don't forget our deal. You want to keep Teddy safe, don't you?"

A chill runs down my spine at the threat to my brother. I thought we were past this, that his safety wasn't in question anymore.

I should have known better.

I turn. "You wouldn't hurt him," I say, but it comes out more like a question than a statement of fact.

Nero's eyes are emotionless and his voice cold as he replies.

"Why not?" he asks. "You said it yourself: I'm a killer. Right?"

Chapter 3

Lily

I try to sleep, but with Nero's threat hanging over me, I barely catch a wink. In the morning, I go through the motions of getting ready for whatever this meeting is: washing and blow-drying my hair, picking out a stylish outfit, and applying makeup to hide the dark shadows under my eyes.

I join Nero downstairs, and head to the foyer.

"Not that exit," he says shortly. He's looking better already, with color in his cheeks, and the bruises on his face giving him a dangerously sexy look.

As if he needed any help with that.

I tear my gaze away. "Why not?"

"We're keeping things undercover, remember?"

He pulls on a baseball cap, low over his eyes, and heads for the back door instead. I follow. At the end of the small garden, there's a gate leading to the back alleyway. Kyle is waiting, behind the wheel of a car I've never seen, a nondescript grey sedan.

"We good?" Nero asks, quickly sliding into the backseat.

"Yeah, there's a guy on the front street, but they didn't spot me. Keep your head down until we're clear."

Nero slumps lower in the seat as we ease out of the alley, and into traffic.

"Little over the top with the cloak and dagger routine, don't you think?" I ask.

Nero glares. "It's for your safety too, you know. Whoever tried to kill me… any of my enemies… They won't hesitate to take you out too, in order to get to me."

I feel a chill. More threats, more enemies. I'm still walking a tightrope here, with a perilous fall waiting on either side.

"I thought that Vance was the one who tried to kill you," I say.

Nero shrugs. "He may have been the one to plant the bomb on the car, but I can't be sure he's actually calling the shots. If Vance is the FBI mole, and I figure he is, I can't understand why he'd try to kill me. The FBI wants to take me down, right? Convict me, not kill me."

"Maybe Vance couldn't help himself," I can't help suggesting. "You bring that out in people."

Nero glares at me, "You'd better hold your tongue when we meet with the Kovacks."

"That's where we're going?" I ask.

He nods. "Word of my death will have spread by now. I need a face-to-face, to reassure them I'm still trying to negotiate our détente. It's been hanging in the balance too long, and I need to make it happen."

"So why bring me?"

"For the charming company, obviously." Nero smirks. I glare back. This is the first time he'd willingly included me in something like this, and I'm not sure I like it. It seems like a dangerous situation, and I can't trust that Nero has my back.

He sighs. "It's a mark of respect to them. But you better act like a good wife, for once."

Wife.

The word lingers as I twist the ring on my left hand. An uncomfortable silence falls as Kyle navigates through traffic. The ride is long, and I wonder where we're going, but I refuse to ask. So, I watch the world glide by outside the windows, until we reach the Long Island suburbs. The neighborhoods are like the one I grew up in, but gradually, the houses grow more lavish, until we turn down a long driveway and pull up outside a opulent, Tudor-style mansion.

We get out of the car, and the front door opens. I recognize one of the men who step out, I saw him meet Nero at the museum in San Francisco. He's with an older gentleman, wearing a suit.

"Igor Kovack, and his nephew," Nero murmurs to me, as we approach the house.

"Barretti, welcome to my home." Igor says, and they greet each other politely. "This must be your lovely wife."

"Hi," I manage a smile. "It's, uh, nice to meet you."

"Please, this way."

Igor leads us into the house, down an impressive hallway to a large formal living room. There are other men waiting there. Large, intimidating men—including the guy who crashed our housewarming party. Sergei. I feel a chill as he sends me a smug grin.

These men are dangerous.

I gulp. Maybe Nero is making a big mistake by coming here. These are sworn enemies, men who have shed blood to try and push the Barrettis out of their turf.

Everyone already thinks he's dead, so what's to stop them from finishing the job?

"This is my wife, Mila," Igor says, gesturing to a dark-haired woman who joins us. He's talking directly to me. "Why don't you enjoy the gardens? They're lovely this time of year."

Translation: get the fuck out.

I glance to Nero. He nods, so I leave them to it.

The doors close behind us, and I shiver with unease.

"Come," Mila says, giving me a serene smile. She clearly has no worries about this meeting. "Would you like a cold drink?"

I think about what Nero said in the car. He needs me to play the part of the perfect wife, so that's what I'll do. "I... Sure. Thank you."

Mila is in her thirties, wearing casual linen pants and a navy blouse that brings out her dark coloring. She stops in the kitchen just long enough to grab a bottle of vodka and two glasses. My eyes widen at the sight of the strong alcohol, but Mila seems unphased. "Forgive the mess," she says, gesturing vaguely at the spotless rooms as we pass. "This was all very last minute, I believe. And the kids... Well, they can make chaos in five minutes flat."

She steps through a pair of open French doors, out to a large patio area. Their garden is huge: The lawn rolls down to a pool, and there's a full playset in the shade, where three kids are currently racing around, yelling and playing together.

Mila leads me to a seating area under a pergola, and opens the vodka. As I take a seat, she pours us each a shot. I sip mine, resisting the urge to shudder at the strong taste.

"Thank you," I say, even as I wish for water.

"Of course. You're our guest." She must sense my nerves, because she offers me a reassuring smile. "They will talk. Just talk. Believe me, Igor would not invite a man under our roof to do him harm. At least, not if he wanted to ever be welcome here again."

"That's... Good to know."

What the hell: I knock back the whole vodka shot, relaxing just a little.

"So..." I search for conversation. I didn't exactly study up on how to talk to a mob wife. My eyes land on the kids again. Safe territory. "How old are they?" I ask.

The children are playing, climbing all over the playset and occasionally calling out for their mother's attention. But they don't need to. She's already watching them. "The girls are five and seven, and my boy is three," she replies proudly. "Do you have children?"

"No, not yet."

She smiles. "They are my greatest blessing."

"But... Don't you worry?" I ask tentatively. I don't want to offend her, but my curiosity is getting the better of me. "I mean, how do you live with the... Uncertainty. Given what your husband... I mean, the way things are?"

Mila pauses. "It's not so bad," she replies finally. "I was raised in this life. My father was in the organization, back in Belgrade. That's how I met Igor," she says with a fond smile.

"And you don't mind, what he does?" I ask, disbelieving.

Mila gives me a knowing look. "His hands may get a little dirty, but whose are clean these days?" she asks. "It's a good life. The kind I dreamed about, back home. We have everything we could need. My children are provided for, they're happy. He takes care of us."

I watch the kids as she speaks, and they certainly do look happy. But they are still so young. They don't know the truth behind this luxurious house, their private school and fancy vacations.

Just like I didn't, back when I was younger.

But the truth came out eventually. Just like it'll come for them. And then what will become of their happiness, their security?

21

A chill runs down my spine, and I realize something. What happens between me and Nero isn't just about my life right now. The choices I make will determine the kind of life that it's possible for me to have.

Do I want children in the future? Yes. I always have. But that was before. Before I found myself in a world of car-bombings and faked death and mafia wars. Real danger surrounding me at every turn. I'm already worried about keeping Teddy safe. I can't imagine putting more innocent lives on the line.

Can I ever have a normal life again? Or am I already in way too deep?

Mila refills my glass, and I drink my vodka, taking comfort in the warmth the alcohol provides. "I heard you have a lovely home," she says, steering the conversation back to safer topics, and we pass the next half-hour with polite chit-chat about home décor, and vacations, and television shows.

Finally, Nero steps out onto the patio. "We can go," he says, giving Mila a respectful nod. "Thank you for keeping my wife entertained."

"Of course," Mila says with a smile. "I hope we will see you again."

"Thank you," I tell her, meaning it. I feel a strange and unexpected comradery with Mila, despite how short our conversation was. She's married to this madness, just like I am now. Our circumstances are different, but we're both connected to powerful and dangerous men. No matter what, that puts a target on our backs.

The question is, can I live with that?

We head home. Nero doesn't say a word. He spends the journey looking deep in thought. We arrive back at the townhouse and sneak in via the back alley again. But once we're safely inside, I can't keep my curiosity at bay.

"So?" I asked, finally breaking the silence. "Are you going to tell me what happened?"

Nero crosses to the bar and pours himself a drink, still moving slowly and carefully after his injuries. But when he turns back around, there's relief on his face.

"The détente is still on. Not only that, but they agreed to help me find Vance."

"How?" I ask, surprised—and relieved. Between the FBI and Vance, we have enough enemies right now. I'm glad the Kovacks aren't on the list.

"They're going to offer a reward, for whoever can claim credit for killing me," Nero says with a grim smile. "A million dollars."

"Wow." I exhale. "That'll be hard for Vance resist."

"And why would he?" Nero agrees. "The world thinks I'm dead. So, Vance will assume there's no danger in collecting his reward."

I have to admit, it's a good plan. "So, what will you—"

The sound of the buzzer interrupts us. Nero freezes, and we exchange a look. "Who is it?" I ask, panicking.

He strides over to the security screen mounted on the wall and lets out a curse. "It's your old friends," he says, grimly. "The FBI."

Chapter 4

Lily

Nero and I remain frozen there for a minute. On the security feed, I can see it's Agent Greggs, and his boss, Agent Lydia Compton. They're waiting impatiently.

"Ignore them." Nero instructs me. "The last thing we need is the feds sniffing around."

But the buzzer sounds, insistent.

"They're not going anywhere." I tell him. "They probably heard about your untimely death," I add. "And I don't have anything to hide from them, remember?"

"Fuck." Nero looks around. "Fine, talk to them. But don't let them back here."

I nod. He slips into the back den and closes the door behind him. Hiding out of sight.

Collecting myself, I walk through to the foyer, and take a deep breath, before opening the front door.

"Mrs. Barretti." Agent Greggs greets me with a sympathetic look. "Sorry to interrupt your afternoon."

"And yet, here you are." I stare back, refusing to show my

emotions. I know the two agents standing on the stoop far too well. Greggs has been trying to get me to turn on Nero since the moment I returned to New York. He was my father's handler, back when he betrayed the Barrettis, and now Greggs is determined to make me follow in his footsteps.

But it's not him I'm worried about.

It's his boss, Lydia, who sends a shiver down my spine. She's the one in charge, running this investigation into Nero with a ferocity that is intimidating, even though I'd never let her know that I thought of her that way.

No, calm and cool is the way to play it with these people.

"Can we come in and talk for a moment?" Greggs asks.

I consider saying no. It's my right to do so. This is my home, after all.

But I know that refusing to let them in the house will just make them suspicious. I'm a grieving widow, I remind myself. I have nothing to hide anymore.

In fact, I should be relieved.

"Sure. Come in."

I step aside, and they follow me into the house.

"We heard about what happened to Nero," Lydia begins, and I brace myself. This woman didn't come to offer her condolences. I'm not sure what she wants, but it's not that.

"We're sorry for your loss," Greggs adds. He seems more sincere, but I'm not falling for it.

"I didn't realize the FBI made home visits for this kind of thing," I say, carefully choosing my words.

Lying to a federal agent is a criminal offense. If they think Nero is dead, then I'm not going to correct them, but I have to tread lightly.

"Well, this is a special case." Greggs adds. "We wanted to check on you, see how you're doing. Given how we left things."

Things... I have to stifle a bitter laugh. That's a funny way of referring to the last time we spoke, when I gave Nero an alibi, and they threatened to take me down with him.

"We know that Nero had some... interesting friends," Lydia adds. "We just wanted to make sure that no one is giving you a hard time. Now that he's gone."

Then I realize, this is a fishing expedition. Nero dying would screw up their whole plan to bust the Barretti organization, so they're still trying to get information out of me, to salvage their investigation.

Well, they won't get a word from me.

"Thank you for your concern," I reply icily. "But I can manage perfectly fine on my own. I've been doing it half my life."

"And you're coping okay with the loss?" Lydia presses, her analytical gaze running over me. "Because frankly, Mrs. Barretti, you don't seem upset."

Her gaze travels, taking in the luxurious townhouse, no doubt filing away every detail. Then she pauses, frowning. I follow her eyeline, and realize to my horror that the drink Nero just poured is still sitting on the sideboard. A whiskey, neat.

Fuck.

I casually stroll over, and pick it up, taking a sip like it's my own. "What's there to be upset about?" I ask, my heart racing. "As you have explained to me many times over, Nero Barretti is a liability. A danger to my safety and my future. Without him, I'll be free to live my life however I want. And you guys will have no reason left to harass me anymore."

"*Was*." Lydia meets my eyes, still narrowed. "Nero was a liability. Past tense."

I knock back the rest of my drink. "Forgive my grammar," I say sarcastically. "It's been a long day. Now, if you'll excuse me..."

I walk back to the front door, and they have no choice but to follow. Still, Greggs lingers.

"If you need to talk. If anything comes up..."

"You'll be the last person I call," I reply, glaring.

"Lily." Lydia gives me a cool nod, and then they leave.

The second they're both out of the house, I slam the door shut and let out a sigh of relief.

Crisis averted, for now.

I rub my forehead, trying to soothe the tension headache forming. In the past twenty-four hours, I've dragged my husband from a car-bomb, faked his death, made small talk with a rival mob wife, and now fended off the feds.

I need a nap, and a drink, not necessarily in that order.

When I return to the living room, Nero is waiting. And from the look on his face, I know he heard everything. It's no surprise that he was listening, but the mix of emotions swirling in his eyes is unexpected.

"Do you mean it?" he asks, voice tight with tension.

"I've lied a hundred times in the past day, you're going to have to be more specific than that."

"What you just told the Feds." Nero says, standing there in the doorway. "That I'm a liability. That you'd be better off without me."

I let out a bitter laugh, refilling his glass and sipping the amber liquid. "What do you think? Look around. My life is chaos now. It's ruined—because of you." My anger rises again, despite my exhaustion. "You destroy everything you touch. Everything would be so much simpler if you were gone. I wouldn't have to hate you like this. I wouldn't have to love—"

I stop myself, but it's too late. Nero's eyes flare. He steps forward.

"What?" he demands. "You wouldn't have to love me?"

I shake my head. I don't want to tell him that I'm still

wrestling with my feelings for him. He doesn't deserve to know that I can't help caring for him, not after everything he's done.

I turn on my heel and walk out, instead. Heading upstairs to my room, where my bags are still half-packed from our fight, days ago.

"Lily," Nero stalks after me. "Where are you going?"

"Away from you," I reply through gritted teeth. I grab more clothes, and stuff them in one of the bags. "I was ready to walk out before the explosion, and I should have. Just left, before you could drag me back into any of *this*."

I go to my drawers and toss toiletries on the bed. Nero grabs my bag and pulls it away.

"You're not going anywhere. We're on lockdown here!"

"We left today." I say stubbornly, still packing.

"Because I had to see Igor, but that was a risk we can't take again." Nero sounds frustrated. "We need to stay, until I figure this out."

"You mean, *you* need to stay here."

"It's for your safety too!" he explodes. "Someone could come after you now that they think I'm not around to protect you. I only trust a small handful of people right now."

"So I'm trapped here?" I yell back. "Gee, why does that sound so familiar? All you've done is keep me captive, bound to you with threats, and lies, and this fucking ring!"

I tear it from my finger and hurl it at him.

Nero doesn't flinch.

"I'm not letting you leave," he says, steely. Blocking the door.

I gulp. Even with him wounded, I'm no match for Nero's brute strength. And I have no doubt he would physically pin me down to keep me from walking out.

The way he's pinned me down before, making me moan. *Making me beg for more.*

"So, what happens now?" I demand, furious at myself for the rush of heat I feel at the memory. "I'm just supposed to do whatever you want?"

Nero stares at me, fire in his eyes. "If you did whatever I wanted, Princess, you'd be on your knees right now, purring all over my cock."

Heat slams through me.

"W-what?" I stammer.

I heard him just fine, but this shift in conversation throws me. My traitorous body is already anticipating the image he's planted in my mind. Getting tighter. *Wetter.*

And Nero sees it. Victory flashes on his face, smug knowledge of just how much power he still wields over me.

"Yeah, that's right." He moves closer, roughly grabbing the bag from my hand and tossing it aside. Eyes still fixed on me. *Hungry.* "You can't help it, can you?" he croons. "Making that sweet little noise in the back of your throat, when I'm fucking it real deep. You can scream and yell at me all you want, but we both know, the minute those knees hit the floor, you'll be begging like a good girl for just one more inch."

My legs go weak, imagining the feel of his hands on me. The rough force that always gets me moaning. The taste of him, dominating me, blocking out the world until there's nothing but my body, and his cock, and all the ways I can service it.

I want it. I want him.

And damn, I hate him for it.

My eyes flicker down to where I can see his erection outlined behind his zipper, growing bigger. Harder.

Nero growls. "Take it out, baby." He moves my hand to cover his groin, pressing down so I'm massaging the huge bulge.

A moan of anticipation slips through my lips. I know what this thick length can do. The heaven it delivers, every damn time.

And Nero knows it, too.

"You don't need to fight me, baby," Nero thrusts against my palm, his breath turning ragged. "At least, not like this. I'll fuck you so good, you never want to leave this house again. You'll stay naked in that bed for me, legs spread, taking it any way I please. I wouldn't even have to tie you down to keep you there, but damn baby, we both know, you'll love it if I do."

I waver, flushed with lust. Because he's right. I *would* love it. He *would* make it good. And I'd let my resistance dissolve in the face of desire. The pleasure he'd provide.

Sex is the most dangerous weapon he wields, and dammit, I surrender every time.

But not now.

With the last shred of my dignity and resolve, I slip under his arm, and duck away from him, putting precious distance between us.

"Get out," I say, pointing to the door. I can't give in to him, no matter how much I want him.

Nero's cocky smirk drops. "Fine. We'll do it your way," he says coldly. "Kyle's guarding the exits. He has my full permission to keep you in this house with whatever means are necessary."

He leaves the room, closing the door behind him with a snap.

I sink back on the bed, my pulse still racing with lust. Dammit. I'm trapped here another night, when I need to be gone. Busy getting far away from Nero—instead of laying here, wound tight, thinking about all his filthy promises.

His hands. His mouth. His cock.

My body thrums like a live wire, and I know, I won't get a moment's peace like this. Not until I find some kind of relief.

He's just down the hallway... A tempting voice whispers in my mind. But I clench my jaw and hike up my skirt instead.

I won't beg him, the way he wants. I won't give him that satisfaction.

But what I do in the privacy of this room...? Well, he doesn't have to know.

I close my eyes, reaching inside my panties to play with my clit. I imagine myself on my knees in front of Nero, just like he told me. His hands roughly grasping my hair. His cock pushing deep into my mouth.

My breath quickens. My fingers rub faster. *Fuck.* In my mind, he's controlling my pace. Pumping in and out, until I'm gasping, and he's close to the edge. But he doesn't finish there, no, he drags me up, and throws me face down on the bed, caging my body, as he yanks my hips up and sinks inside me from behind.

I roll over, burying my face in the pillows as I imagine him bucking into me. Fingers digging into my thighs, the sharp snap of his hips as he sets a punishing rhythm. I sink a finger inside myself, and then another, but it's nowhere near enough. I whimper in frustration, bucking against my hand.

I need him, thick inside me. Filling me up.

My breathing grows heavy, and I bite my lip to hold in a moan. I don't want Nero to hear. If he knows what I'm doing, he'll know he got under my skin.

I can't give him that victory over me.

But damn, a part of me wants him to know. A part of me wants him to come into the room and ravage me.

Drag me over the edge of pleasure, the way only he knows how.

I move my fingers faster and faster, my palm pressed against my clit, providing just enough friction to send electric waves of pleasure through me. It's a pale imitation of Nero's electrical charge, but *fuck*, it gets me there, just. I come in a ripple, my back arching and my heart beating wildly against my ribcage.

I slump down, spent—but not feeling any of the relief I was craving. Because my own hands can't ever compare to what he does to me. Hell, the best sex toys in the world couldn't measure up.

And then the sound of slow applause comes from across the room.

I sit up, whirling around—to see Nero standing there in the now-open doorway. Clapping me. Mocking.

"That was quite a show, Princess," he smirks. "Now, are you nice and warmed up for the real deal?"

Humiliation flushes, hot in my veins. "Get out!" I scream. I grab the nearest object, and throw it at him. The water glass smashes against the doorway by his head. "Get the hell out!"

"You know where to find me." Nero backs up, and shuts the door behind him, but his laughter echoes all the way down the hall.

I jump up and lock the door behind him this time. But I know, it's not to keep him out.

It's to stop me from looking for him.

Chapter 5

Nero

It doesn't take long for the reward gambit to work. Whatever reasons Vance had to try and kill me, I know he won't be able to resist claiming the credit, when that credit comes with a million bucks as a sweetener.

Sure enough, I'm meeting with Chase and Miles at the house when the call comes through.

"What I want to know, is who put him up to it?" Miles is asking. "Your father sent him. He was supposed to be a loyal Barretti man."

"Did ten years in lockup, never once rolled," Chase agrees. "Why the fuck does a guy like that turn around and try and take you out? It doesn't make sense."

I see the number and snatch up my phone, holding up my hand to gesture for them to quiet.

"Yeah?" I bark.

"He surfaced.' Igor doesn't fuck around with small talk. "Our guys put it around that the money was waiting, as a sign of our gratitude. He contacted a friendly party, made it clear he wants to collect."

I nod, glancing to Miles and Chase. They're watching curiously, only able to hear my side of the conversation. I didn't share details of this particular play—and Chase still doesn't know I'm negotiating with our sworn enemies. He'd hit the roof if he knew.

"You have a meet scheduled yet?" I ask carefully.

"Tonight. Eight p.m. Louie's bar, downtown. I take it you'll handle it from here?"

"I'll send someone. And... Thank you. I appreciate this."

Igor sounds amused. "See now, Mr. Barretti, a little friendship can go a long way."

I hang up. Friendship? I don't trust Igor for a second. The man is a ruthless killer—just like me. But right now, our interests are aligned. We've been working on a deal to hand over Barretti territory and assets to his people, so it's in his best interest to keep me alive, long enough to continue our negotiations.

Negotiations that will have the Barrettis exiting the organized crime game for good.

I've been trying to take us legit for years now, away from the murder and mayhem, and into the real money. Real estate. Investments. I pulled off a massive development deal with a land parcel downtown, and we've already broken ground on construction for luxury retail and apartments. Those things print so much money, our criminal activities are small fry in comparison. Finally, a way out of the crime business is within my grasp.

If I can stop any more explosions—literal or otherwise—blowing it all to shit.

"What's going on, boss?" Miles asks.

"I have a lead on Vance," I say, my gaze shifting to Chase.

"A lead? From where?" Chase asks.

"A reliable source," I reply, keeping it vague. "He'll be at

Louie's. Tonight at eight. You should be there to have a word," I tell Chase meaningfully.

He gets to his feet. "Oh, you can count on it. We'll have a whole damn conversation. In fact—"

Miles coughs loudly. "As your lawyer, I should remind you, we may be questioned about this conversation. By officers of the law."

Chase snorts. "Like I said, we'll talk."

"Just make sure you have the last word," I add, as Miles sighs again, muttering about plausible deniability. The guy's a good lawyer, but who are we kidding? I may not say the words out loud, but Chase knows his assignment:

Make sure Vance doesn't live to come after me again.

Chase exits, but Miles stays behind. He waits a moment after Chase is out the door before speaking.

"So... When are you planning to tell Chase about the détente with the Kovacks?"

I sigh, leaning back in my chair. "Soon. He's not going to be happy. You know Chase is tied to the old way of doing things. Things are volatile enough as it is, the last thing I need is him kicking up a fuss about the deal."

Miles makes a face. "Don't leave it too late," he warns me. "Shit's gonna hit the fan one way or another."

"Yeah. I just don't need it spraying all over an open blaze," I reply, then chuckle. "Or some other damn metaphor."

Miles stands, and I notice the guy doesn't look so great. Dark circles under his eyes, and he looks pale, too. "You holding up OK?" I ask.

He flinches. "What? Yeah, sure. Just... Hearing you were dead took a few years off my life, that's all."

"I'm sorry I couldn't warn you sooner," I say.

"I get it," he nods. "But Avery... She wasn't impressed, to say the least."

"Oh, she made that clear," I say, recalling the absolute earful I got the other day when I came clean to her about faking my death. "My ears are still ringing. That girl has a mouth like a fucking sailor."

"Yeah, she does," Miles says with an affectionate smile.

I notice, but I let it slide. Something's been brewing between the two of them for a while, but hell if I'm going to stick my nose in. They've both been loyal to me my whole life, and part of the reason I'm trying to take this organization legit is to protect them, too. Give them a shot at a decent life, away from all this violence.

"Let me know when you're going to leak it, if you're still standing," Miles says, heading for the front door. "I can delay the stuff like probate and inheritance for a while longer, but somebody's going to ask questions soon, and want to see a death certificate. Or a funeral."

I nod. "Will do."

"And, as your lawyer..." Miles pauses. "I suggest you have a damn good alibi tonight. Around eight." He gives me a look.

Vance.

"You mean, better than being dead?" I give a hollow laugh. "Yeah, don't worry. I'm not stepping foot outside this house just yet."

"Good."

Miles heads out, and as the door closes behind him, I hear Lily's footsteps, light on the stairs. She's barefoot in a sundress, her damp hair twisted up on the top of her head.

"Let me guess, we're still on lockdown." Stopping just a few feet away, she puts her hands on her hips, and the fire in her eyes makes me want to put her in her place. Preferably with a combination of punishment and mind-blowing pleasure. "How much longer are you going to keep me prisoner in this place?

I'm missing my art classes," she adds, a note of genuine hurt in her voice.

Damn, I forgot about those—and how much they mean to her. But I'm not risking her safety over a couple of classes.

"You can make up the credits," I tell her, heading back towards my office.

She trails after me. "I'll fail the semester."

"So I'll write a fucking check and they'll pass you."

"That's your answer to everything, isn't it?" Lily demands, and when I turn back, she's standing there, cheeks flushed with anger. "Money—or a bullet."

"Well, yeah," I drawl, knowing it'll get her even madder. "Tell me a problem I can't solve with either of them. Or my cock," I add. "That's the solution you love best, isn't it, Princess?"

She flushes deeper, looking just the way she did laying on that bed last night, grinding the pillows in search of release.

"To hell with your big plans, maybe you should just stay dead," she tells me furiously. "Believe me, nobody will miss you."

Whirling on her heel, she goes upstairs to her studio and slams the door behind her. I know she's locked it behind her. Hell, I'd be surprised if she didn't barricade it too, after the show she accidentally gave me last night.

I go pour a drink and swallow a couple of the painkillers the doctor gave me. I'm hiding it from my guys and Lily, but my body still aches from the explosion, reminding me just how close I came to death. How I made it out of there, I'm still not sure. I don't remember what happened, just flashes of Lily, holding me close, screaming at me to hold on and keep breathing.

But that's impossible, she wasn't even there.

And she sure as hell wouldn't have saved me if she had been, she's made that perfectly clear.

So, I don't know what I was seeing. My guardian angel, maybe. Keeping me from slipping away.

You should just stay dead...

Lily's words echo, and I take a moment to think about what she said.

What if I didn't reappear when Vance is dealt with? Everybody already thinks I'm gone. What if I let them keep believing it?

The thought is a tempting one. I could start over, leave all this bullshit behind and go somewhere that nobody even knows the Barretti name. And if I took Lily with me...

We could be free.

She'd be safe. I'd be happy. It sounds pretty damn good to me.

But I sigh. I know it's just a fantasy. I can try to change things here in New York but running away isn't really an option. I'll always be who I am. It's in my blood.

I'll be a Barretti until the day I die.

A noise startles me out of my daydreams. I reach for a gun automatically, but stop when I see who just walked in.

"Avery." I exhale. "Who gave you keys?"

"I'm not going to stand around and ring the doorbell," she snaps, still clearly pissed at me. "What are you going to do, come answer the door so anyone can see?"

She walks past me, into my office, pulling a stack of paperwork from her bag. "I need signatures," she says, when I join her. "Everything's backdated, before your tragic death. Should keep things running a while longer."

"Good thinking," I nod. I don't know what I'd do without her around to run our legitimate businesses. She's one of my most valuable assets.

And a friend I can rely on.

I start flipping through the stack of papers she brought as she sits in the seat in front of the desk and waits. I scrawl my signature on the dotted lines without really reading anything. By now, I can trust that every report is just fine. Avery is good at this sort of thing.

"Lily talking to you yet?" she asks.

"Define 'talking'," I reply with a rueful scowl.

"Yeah, well you owe her your thanks—and an apology. She was really shaken up."

"From what?" I look up. "She thought I was dead for all of five seconds before busting into the room."

Avery gives me an odd look. "I'm talking about before that. When the bomb went off. Thank God she followed you to the meeting," she adds. "Guess she figured out Vance was dangerous and decided to warn you."

I stop dead. "Wait... What?" I demand. Lily followed me? "She was there?"

Avery furrows her brow. "You didn't know? She's the one who saved you," she explains. "She gave CPR, got you breathing again. If she hadn't been around... You wouldn't have made it."

I sit down, stunned. I thought that I imagined Lily crying out my name, pressing her lips to mine. I thought it was my mind producing the only thing that could really provide me with comfort when I was so close to death.

I was wrong.

"I had no idea," I say quietly. "She never mentioned it."

Avery lets out a low whistle. "OK, you're really going to have to grovel," she smirks. "Buy something expensive. Really expensive."

I continue signing the papers without further comment, but

my mind is racing. We finish up, and Avery lets herself out, but I'm still turning the information over in my mind.

Lily saved me.

For days, she's been spitting mad. Saying she wished I had died in the explosion, that I deserved to suffer for everything I've done. I know finding out about the murder of her mother changed everything between us, and I thought that rift was permanent. That there was no hope of ever repairing the damage and getting back to the trust and happiness we'd found.

But she saved me.

Why?

I storm upstairs to Lily's art studio. The door is still locked, so I ball my fist and bang it against the wooden surface with thundering blows.

"Open up, Princess!"

She ignores me at first, but I'm a persistent man, and she eventually unlocks the door, yanking it open.

"What?" she snaps.

I look at her, and know that the anger is just a front. She may spit insults and threats at me, but her actions speak louder than words. She came to warn me, to protect me. She begged me not to die.

She gave me the air from her own lungs to try and keep me breathing.

She's mine.

"Enough," I growl, stalking into the room. "You don't hate me, so quit pretending like you do."

"I'm not pretending," she protests.

"Oh yeah?" I close the distance between us, taking her face in both my hands. "Tell that to your body, Princess. Because it's been aching for me for days."

She gives an involuntary shiver, her nipples going hard

through the thin cotton of her dress. She flushes. "It doesn't mean anything. It's just hormones."

"Say that again," I demand, on edge. I've been wound tight for days now, keeping my distance. Waiting for her to break first and come begging at my door.

But I'm done waiting.

"*This* is just hormones?" I grab her by the waist, pulling her in until her body is flush against mine. She gasps, her hands going to my chest, but she doesn't push me away. "How about *this*?"

I trail a hand over her chest, palming one delicious breast in my hand. Pinching her nipple until she moans.

"Why are you fighting this so damn hard?" I demand, my breath ragged at her nearness. I'm already hard against her, so close to being buried deep where I belong. "Why can't you admit it? You're angry because you were scared. Scared of losing me."

"N—no..." Lily's denial is barely a whisper. Her eyes glaze with lust as she tilts her head back to look up at me. "I wasn't scared..." her lie trails off, her breath catching as I lick up the side of her neck, making her shudder in my arms. "*Nero...*"

She can't admit it, not even to herself, but there's a plea in her voice now. One I won't leave unanswered.

I'm done playing around and teasing her. I need a taste of her sweetness.

My mouth claims hers, hot and hard, and she sinks against me, all pretense at resistance melting away under the force of our passion. Her hands go up around my neck, and she presses closer, making little mewling noises as my tongue plunders her mouth.

But fuck, it's nowhere near enough.

I pick her up and carry her to the couch in the corner of the room, shoving her roughly back on the cushions. Thank fuck she's wearing a sundress, I only need to push the skirt up around her waist to reveal the strip of damp panties, and then I tear them away, too.

I don't take my time. There's no going slow and easy when I'm this hungry for her.

"Open wide, baby," I growl, sinking to my knees. "I've been starving for a taste."

Lily's legs part for me as if of their own accord, and I can't keep the smirk off my face as I lean in. The movement makes my bruised ribs ache in protest, but I ignore it.

Some things are worth a little pain.

She watches me, breathless, eyes bright and wild. "I'm still mad at you," she manages, her voice shaking.

"So be mad, baby." I run my palms up the inside of her thighs, the skin soft and warm. I spread her even wider and let out a small growl at the sight of her cunt glistening for me. "Punish me with this sweet pussy. Get yourself off on my tongue."

I lean in and lap at her clit, working it in a small circle. Lily's gasp is like sweet music to my ears.

"Yeah, you sound real good and mad," I gloat, as she lets out a whimper.

I want to tease her about how quickly she's changed her tune, but I've got more important things in mind. Instead, I flatten my tongue and go hard, exploring her folds and lapping up her sweetness.

My cock is hard as steel, straining my pants. Before long, I'm devouring her pussy like a starving man, making her buck against me and gasp. Her fingers plunge into my hair, holding on as I suck her clit, flicking my tongue over the sensitive nub.

"Nero!" she cries out, writhing against me. "Oh god!"

That's right, baby. I thrust two fingers inside, and pump them, just the way she likes, as my tongue keeps up its relentless attack on her sensitive nub. It's not long before her body is arching, and she lets out a cry of pure pleasure.

"There! Fuck, don't stop! Don't—*Ahhhhh!*"

She comes screaming, her body clenching against me. It's hot as hell, a goddamn work of art.

But I'm not done yet.

I rise to my feet again, stripping open my jeans. She's splayed there on the cushions, breathless and flushed. A goddess.

My wife.

"Didn't seem so mad when you were coming all over my tongue, did you now, Princess?" I ask, taking out my cock. Fuck, I'm straining for her, thick and heavy in my hand as I prepare to claim what's mine. "Lie to me all you want, but at least be honest with yourself about how you really feel."

The hazy satisfaction drains out of Lily's face. She sits up, suddenly yanking her dress back into place.

"Don't pat yourself on the back," she spits, all fury again. "You're not the only guy who's ever gotten me off. Hell, I've got toys that made me come harder. And they didn't bore me with a play-by-play," she adds, scrambling to her feet.

She pushes past me and walks out, leaving me standing there, horny as hell, with my cock in my hand.

Goddammit!

I have to laugh at her guts. She's still putting up a good front about hating me, but I know the truth now. I remember the way she cradled my body in her lap after the explosion, whispering prayers and promises, all the way home.

I'm not giving up on us, not by a long shot. I'm going to show her that she still belongs to me.

Just like I belong to her, completely.

But right now? I need a fucking cold shower.

Chapter 6

Lily

I don't know how, and I definitely don't want to know why, but Nero curtly informs me I can leave the house again and go back to art school. Something has changed, and I can only assume that Vance is out of the picture now. Nero's plan to use the Kovack reward as bait must have worked and drawn him out of hiding.

And whatever happened to Vance next...? Well, I don't ask any questions. Something tells me that I'm better off not knowing the answer.

After all the drama of the past few days, it's a relief to be back on campus again, just another student in the crowds. I catch up on my classes and check in with my tutors, pretending I've been sick to explain my absence. I'm pleased to learn that while I was away, I didn't miss much in my drawing class, where we're starting a new still life project.

"Focus on the line work," my teacher tells us, as we settle in front of a display of potted plants. "Think about shape, not just what's there, but the absence of form, too. Negative space."

"Sure," the student beside me mutters. "Because it's so easy drawing what *isn't* there."

I smile. "You think if we turn in a blank sheet, she'll accept it?"

He grins. "Dare you to try it."

"Oh no, not me. I've already missed enough, I'll fail for sure."

"That's right," he studies me. "You haven't been around this week."

I clear my throat. "Flu," I lie again, and it rolls easily off my tongue this time.

"Aww man, that sucks." He grimaces. "Hope you're feeling better."

I nod and turn back to my easel. I exhale, trying to focus every bit of my attention on the assignment. I need a break from the outside world, but the quiet of the room allows my thoughts to roam free, and I can't stop thinking about Nero.

His hands, pressing me down on the couch cushions. The feel of his mouth, relentless against me. The look in his eyes, positioned there between my thighs: victory mingling with pure unleashed desire.

I shudder, flushing hotly all over again.

"Lie to me all you want, but at least be honest with yourself about how you really feel."

He was speaking the truth, of course. My body doesn't hate him at all. Nor does my heart. Even now, just the memory of watching him lower his head between my legs makes my blood run wild, pounding in my veins.

I wish he didn't know the effect he has on me, but I also can't hide it. The chemistry between us is too strong.

And as for the hold he has on my emotions...

"Ah, Lily, good to have you back with us."

I look up from my drawing to see that the teacher has made

her way over to me. She's looking down, measuring my progress with a speculative look. I give her a strained smile.

"I guess I might be overthinking this," I say, knowing that I should be further along in the process by now. Class is already almost over, and with my wandering thoughts, I've barely completed half the scene.

"Thinking might be your problem," she says, with a knowing smile. "Artists can become crippled by their own thoughts, questioning every line they draw, every stroke of the paintbrush. You have to just trust your instincts."

I nod. "Thanks. I'll try."

She moves on, but her words linger.

Trust your instincts.

She's right. I produce my best art when I'm doing that, when I can just shut off the voices of doubt and reason in my mind, and give myself over to the project. I know deep down what brushstrokes I should use, the sense of light and color in a painting, and the more I have confidence in those choices and stop second-guessing, the better a piece always is.

So what am I supposed to do when it comes to my instincts about Nero?

In my heart, I know we belong together, but I've been fighting that instinct since the day he found me again. Even after everything we've been through, being drawn back to him time and time again, I still have this voice in my head that tells me it's a mistake. That I shouldn't want him.

Shouldn't *need* him, the way I need oxygen. Beyond rational thought.

I've been going around and around, back and forth, warring between my head and my heart all this time. And just when I think I've made a decision, the scales tip again. Because Nero moves them, through sheer force of his will.

I know I can't go on like this much longer. I know that soon, I'll have to make the final choice.

But which of my instincts will win out?

After class is over, I pack up my supplies. The student beside me, Chris, screws his paper into a ball and tosses it in the trash as we leave the classroom.

"Why did you do that?" I protest. "It was looking great."

"It was a mess," he corrects me, laughing good-naturedly. "And I'm a perfectionist. If it's not how I picture it, I tear the whole thing up and start again."

"What would our teachers say?" I tease. "It's the process. The art of failure."

"Ah yes, the one discipline I *have* learned," he jokes, and I laugh.

"Come on. Literally every artist in history has created crappy first drafts. Even Monet," I add. "All those sketches of the waterlilies? You would never have guessed they'd turn into a masterpiece, one day."

"So you're a Monet girl," he remarks, as we walk out of the building and into the bright sunlight. "I should have guessed."

"Is that predictable?"

"No." he smiles. "I love him, too. But I think my favorite would have to be Renoir, though. His work had a lot of influence on the development of Impressionist style."

"Yes! And have you seen some of his later works?" I ask. "He was so talented at capturing feminine beauty. *Grandes Baigneuses* or *Girls at the Piano*… They are amazing."

"I saw *Grandes Baigneuses* in person at the Philadelphia Museum of Art a few years ago."

I gasp. "Okay, I'm officially jealous."

He smiles. "Every time I visit a new city, I always go to as many museums as I can. There's nothing I'd rather do. My girlfriend gets so bored, I drag her around every gallery in town."

I'm laughing when I catch sight of Nero, across the quad. He's walking fast towards us, glaring. Chris tenses up beside me, and I don't blame him. Nero is an imposing man at the best of times.

And from the look on his face, now is not a good time.

"Nero, hi," I say, confused. "What are you doing here? Is something wrong?"

I'm worried there's been a new development, some reason he came to collect me in person. But Nero's focus is entirely on Chris.

"Does a husband need a reason to come meet his *wife?*" Nero drapes his arm around my shoulder in a possessive gesture. He's marking his territory, caveman-style.

Chris shifts his weight uncomfortably from one foot to the other. "Well, I guess I'll go," he says.

"You do that," Nero says rudely.

"See you in class!" I add with a smile, trying to make up for Nero's caveman routine.

"Let's go," he snaps, practically dragging me away. He stalks toward the parking lot at a fast pace, and I have to almost jog to keep up with his long stride.

He opens the passenger door of his car. "Get in."

I do as he says, not wanting to have a fight here in the parking lot for everyone to see. I've been embarrassed enough today already. But all bets are off as Nero gets in behind the wheel and starts to drive us home.

"What the hell was that all about?" I finally explode.

"I could ask you the same question," Nero growls out, leaning on the horn. "Are you seeing someone else, like art boy back there?"

My jaw drops. Is he out of his mind? Since when would I even have time to see anybody else, even if I wanted to?

But his distrust stings. After everything we've been through... My anger makes me reply archly, "What if I am?"

"Knock it off, Lily," he snarls. "It's not funny."

"Who says I'm kidding?" I retort, settling back in my seat. If he wants to make ridiculous accusations, he'll need to live with the consequences. "I've been cooped up in that house with you far too much, but that doesn't mean I can't take a lover. Someone who can worship my body the way I deserve."

Nero doesn't reply, but his hands tighten on the steering wheel until his knuckles turn white.

"I'm sure he could make me feel special, making me come over and over again," I muse, enjoying this now. "And maybe I would pick someone at school, it would be so convenient, don't you think? We could do it right there in the classroom after everyone else has left. I'd let him bend me over the desk and—"

"Enough!" Nero roars.

I fall silent, quietly satisfied with the idea that I've pushed him to the edge. I'm playing with fire here, I know. After all, if he said these things about another woman, taunted me with the idea of him cheating...?

I don't know what I'd do. But it wouldn't be pretty.

We ride back home in silence, electricity crackling in the air between us, slowly igniting the heat in my veins.

He's jealous. *Good.* He's angry at the idea of me with another man. *Even better.* Maybe it's fucked up, but I want him to think about the idea of losing me. He hasn't taken the idea seriously yet, assuming he can keep me locked down. That this ring on my finger somehow will keep me here no matter what.

Would he even care if I left?

It doesn't make any sense, but I desperately want the answer to be 'yes,' which is why, when we pull up at the house, I take my time getting out of the car, and walk to the front door slowly, swaying my hips. I throw a glance over my shoulder.

Nero's face is stormy. My pulse kicks.

"Get in the house, Princess," he says in a low voice.

I shiver, anticipation blooming low in my belly. Nero is sexy as hell any day of the week, but when he's looking at me like that, like he wants to burn the whole world down just to get to me?

I can't resist it. I never have.

The minute we're inside, Nero picks me up, and throws me over his shoulder, striding through to the living room.

"Put me down!" I yelp, upside down. "Nero!"

"If you're going to act like a brat, I'll damn well treat you like one."

Nero dumps me unceremoniously on the couch and pulls me across his lap. I'm still breathless with surprise, face down in the cushions, when he yanks my dress up over my ass. He grabs my panties and there's a ripping sound in the air as the delicate lace fabric gives way.

Then he lands a stinging smack on my bare ass.

I yelp again, jolting forward with surprise at the impact.

"This is what you get for taunting me in the car," he growls, delivering a second smack. "For even imagining yourself with another man."

I wriggle. "You don't own me," I throw back at him, furious and turned on now, all at the same time.

Nero's eyes are blazing. One hand is rough, tangled in my hair, holding me down as the other lands a fresh spank against the sensitive skin of my bare ass.

"No, I don't," he growls, sounding tormented. "But you own me. Dammit, Lily, why do you have to make this so damn hard?"

He smacks me again, and I can feel him hard, alright. Bulging against me, a temptation I don't want to ignore.

It's been hell, resisting him these past few days. All I want is him inside me, the precious moments where the world disappears, and it's only our bodies that matter, coming together in our explosive dance.

It's the only time the doubts and questions fade. The only time everything makes sense.

When I belong to him.

He spanks me again, and a moan slips from my lips. My desire is skyrocketing with every punishing stroke. I shouldn't like this. But fuck, I do. I'm sure my ass is red right now, and I wonder if Nero is enjoying this as much as I am.

I wriggle on his lap, deliberately, and hear a groan sound.

Good.

I arch back, presenting my ass this time. "Go on," I demand breathlessly. "Punish me if you want. But we both know, you wouldn't want me any other way. You love it when I push back," I say, twisting to meeting his eyes behind my shoulder. "I'm the only one who fights you. The only one who won't bow down to the big bad Nero Barretti."

Nero groans again, ragged. "Lily..."

Just when I think he's going to land another blow on my ass, he brings his hand lower, slipping it through my slick folds. My legs are already parted, my body silently begging for him to give me what I need.

"You're right, Princess," Nero's voice is tortured. "Fuck, you're always right."

His fingers find my entrance, and he slowly thrusts two inside me. My hands tighten into fists on the couch as he starts to pump them in and out of my wet entrance. "I'm addicted to you, baby," he growls. "To this tight pussy, fuck, the way you clench it for me, like a goddamn vice."

I moan again, pressing back against his hand. Needing him deeper. God, I can feel myself barreling toward my climax, the real release that's been eluding me for days.

But Nero senses it coming too, and pulls away. He lifts me off his lap, and stands, leaving me gasping there on the couch with my skirt rucked up around my waist.

"What...?" I gasp, still aching. "Nero, please..."

He looks down at me, and I see his expression change. The control shifting back over his features, until he's in charge, all over again. "Not so fun, when you're the one left hanging, is it?" he asks with a smirk.

I let out a noise of frustration, realizing this is payback for the way I walked out on him the other night, and left him hard and horny for me. My hand moves between my thighs to chase the glimpse of pleasure.

"No." Nero's voice is steely, stopping me in my tracks. "This time, you're going to be the one who waits." His smile turns teasing, full of power—and revenge. "I'm taking you to dinner, just like this. Wet and panting for me. So you can feel my handprint with every step, and remember, I'll always give you what you deserve... Whether you like it or not."

Chapter 7

Lily

Nero gets his wish. My ass is sore from his spanking, and it stings with every step. Reminding me how roughly he handled me.

And how I want *more*.

"So, I guess laying low is officially over," I comment as Nero pulls up in front of one of the hottest new restaurants in town. It's owned by some celebrity chef that's known for throwing things in the kitchen, yelling at his staff, and creating some of the best food in the world.

"It's not necessary anymore," Nero replies with a nod. "Vance won't be causing any more trouble for me."

I know what that means, and I don't want the details. Although, when I think about the horror I felt when that car bomb went off, I can't allow myself to feel bad about it.

The valet opens my door as Nero steps out on the other side, handing over his car keys. I have to admit to myself that he looks amazing tonight, filling out the black suit he's wearing just right. He's wearing a cocky smirk that reminds me of sex. It's the way he looks when he knows he's brought me to the brink of pleasure.

"Well, you certainly know how to make an entrance," I say as we walk into the restaurant.

We haven't even made it to the hostess stand yet, and heads are turning, people are whispering to each other, and a few cell phones come out to snap a picture or two. It looks like news of Nero Barretti's survival is causing quite a stir.

And that was probably his intention. He's announcing himself as alive in a big way by bringing us here. News will probably spread throughout the city of his return before we've even had our appetizers.

"What can I say?" Nero gives a casual shrug, slinging his arm around my shoulder. "I've learned a thing or two about being in the spotlight from parading around at those high-society events with you on my arm."

We approach the hostess stand, where he doesn't even need to announce his name before we're whisked to a table. It's the best in restaurant, on a platform near the window, where we have a nice view of a park across the street. It's nice to spot a slice of green in this city of concrete and steel.

"It's still surprising to me that you eat at places like this," I can't resist saying. "I remember back when you thought buying a girl a hot dog from a street cart was a good idea."

Nero smiles. "You want to talk about how I've changed, but what about you? That street cart was your idea of an adventure back then."

"Oh, to be that young again."

"Are you kidding me? I wouldn't want to be a teenager these days."

"Life is rough for them, isn't it?"

"No. I mean, teenagers are dumb."

I laugh. I can't help it. "A lot of people think that about the younger generations."

"Then, I guess I'm a crotchety old man."

I roll my eyes, but I'm smiling.

The menu is small, with no prices listed, telling me it's expensive and the food is going to be amazing. When the waitress comes, Nero orders a bottle of wine for us, and we place our orders. When we're alone again, I look at Nero across the candlelit table, and feel a pang.

"What are we really doing here?" I ask softly.

"Announcing my miraculous survival," he replies.

"No. You could have done that anywhere, with anyone," I shake my head. "But you took me on a date, instead. You always have an ulterior motive," I remind him. "So tell me what's going on?"

Nero is silent a moment, then he sighs. "I know the past week hasn't been easy for you," he says, and when he meets my eyes, I see the honesty there. "I wanted to do something nice, that's all. A regular date."

I pause, my heart aching. Nothing about life with Nero is regular, but I understand the urge. To reclaim a few moments of calm amongst the chaos. To just be *us*.

"Regular..." I say, relaxing. "Does that mean small talk about the weather?"

He chuckles. "Baby, we can talk about anything you want."

"Even bad reality TV?" I tease.

"Please. Go right ahead."

We chat while we wait for the food, although I find that I'm doing most of the talking. I decide not to torment him with a rundown of the latest Netflix shows I've been watching to try and fall asleep. Instead, I tell him all about my art classes, carefully avoiding the topic of Chris and what happened earlier today. It's easy to talk about my paintings, the current ones I'm working on and the ideas I have for future projects.

The food arrives, and we dig in.

"Good?" Nero asks.

I nod. My starter is a scallop carpaccio, and I can't help sighing with satisfaction as I take a bite. It's amazing.

"Careful," Nero's voice is smoky. "I'll get jealous. I only want you making that kind of noise for me."

My eyes meet his and there's a familiar bolt of heat. My core is already aching from the unfulfilled pleasure I was so close to earlier, and just this one look makes me hungry for more.

"So be jealous," I tease, lightening the tone. I tear my eyes away from his, taking a sip of my wine. I hope it can cool me off. "Because I haven't even gotten started on dessert."

Nero chuckles—and then stops, his eyes narrowing at something behind me.

I turn, just as Agent Lydia Compton appears at our table. "How romantic," she says, looking back and forth between us. "Just a couple of lovebirds out on the town. Celebrating anything special?"

I tense, as she pulls out a chair and takes a seat. Her smile is tight and doesn't reach her eyes.

Nero doesn't seem rattled, though. He just picks up his wine glass and takes a sip as he leans back in his chair, as if he doesn't have a care in the world. "Agent Compton," he says, smiling dangerously. "You're quite a ways from the downtown office. Did you have a reservation? I'm sure I can arrange one if you need."

Lydia stares back. "We were told you were dead."

Nero shrugs. "I'm afraid that reports of my death have been grossly exaggerated."

"And what about your friend, Vance?" Lydia demands.

"I've been meaning to have a chat with him, but he seems to be missing."

Nero smirks. "Maybe he's on a bender somewhere. I don't keep track of these things."

Lydia seethes, as Nero gestures to the hostess. "Now, if you don't mind, you can direct any further inquiries to my attorney. I'm trying to enjoy a meal with my wife."

Lydia turns her attention to me. "You know, Mrs. Barretti, lying to a federal agent is a crime."

"Really?" I play it cool, too, even as her presence rattles me. "I don't remember lying."

"When we came to discuss your husband's death—"

"—I never said he was dead," I interrupt. "In fact, you'll remember I talked about him in the present tense." I force a smile. "You're the one who jumped to conclusions. Which you've been doing an awful lot lately, don't you think?"

"This is serious." She scowls. "I could charge you with obstruction of justice. You know that we have an active investigation against the Barretti crime organization—"

"You have no proof that any such thing exists," Nero interrupts. Now, he sounds annoyed. She's found a way to push his buttons. "If you did, you'd use it to make arrests. Who knows, maybe your mole was just stringing you along?"

"And you killed him for it."

"That's a bold accusation, and I have no idea what you're talking about." Nero's voice turns icy and he glares across the table. "You're making quite a scene, Agent Compton, and I'd prefer to enjoy my meal in peace. It turns out that dying gives you an appetite."

Lydia seems to realize that she's not going to rattle us. She slowly gets to her feet and gives a shrug. "Enjoy the meal. Prison food leaves a lot to be desired. As I'm sure your father would agree."

She walks out, and I watch her go, not relaxing until I see her leave the restaurant. When she's finally gone, Nero lifts his glass.

"A toast," he says, "to the end of that little problem."

"Are you sure that's the end of it?" I ask, swallowing hard. "She seems to think differently."

"She's got nothing." He says it confidently. "The FBI isn't going to let her keep chasing after me with nothing to show for it. It's why she showed up here, she's getting desperate. I'll have Miles cause a fuss tomorrow, file for harassment. They'll have to back off—for a while, at least."

A while...

Because that's all the reprieve we're going to get. And even if Lydia does take a break from coming after us, that's only one of Nero's problems right now.

Nero smiles. "So, how about dessert?"

I nod, and force a smile for the rest of dinner, but the relaxed mood is gone. By the time we get home, I have a tight sadness lodged in my gut, more grief than any anger or resentment against him.

Will we ever get a regular date night, just the two of us?

Can we ever escape the chaos that always seems to loom overhead, dark clouds threatening storms at any moment?

Back the house, I pause a moment in the foyer, then turn to head upstairs.

"Where are you going?"

Nero's voice makes me pause on the stairs.

"To bed," I reply quietly.

He looks up at me, and when he speaks, his voice is ringing with emotion. "Is this how it's going to be now? You locking yourself in that guestroom, pretending like... Like we're not *us*!"

I swallow, suddenly on the edge of tears. Anger was easier

than this. At least with rage, I had something to hold onto. A way to defend against the ache in my heart.

Against loving him.

"How else can it be?" I ask hopelessly, but I don't wait for his reply. I go up to the guest room, but I'm not surprised when I hear his footsteps following. I feel his presence behind me in the doorway as I kick off my shoes and take my hair down. His eyes on me, watching.

Finally, he speaks. "If there's really no hope for us, why did you save me?"

I whirl around. "W-what are you talking about?"

Nero takes a step closer, his eyes burning with intensity. "I know that you came after me that night, and that you gave me CPR. I know that you saved my life," he says harshly, faced etched with ragged emotion. "So, the question is, why did you bother? If you hate me so much, why fight to keep me alive?" he demands. "Why beg me not to leave you, if you can't wait to get away?"

"Because I had to!" I explode, everything that I felt that night surging up to the surface again, in great waves of confusion and desperation. "I couldn't let you die," I yell. "I couldn't face a world without you in it. You think I want to need you like this? I can't stand it, but I do! Just like I can't stop loving you!"

There's a beat of silence, as Nero stares at me. His face changing. The frustration and bitterness melting away, until he looks almost like the boy I used to know.

The one who loved me more than anything.

"Lily—" he starts towards me.

I flinch back, on the edge here. Knowing I could fall.

"Lily, it's OK." He keeps coming, until he's standing right in front of me, tilting my face up, despite my tears. "Shh," he whispers, caressing my face. "I can't stop loving you either."

His words are my undoing. His words—and the look in his eyes.

And then we're reaching for each other, colliding in a passionate kiss, full of longing and regret. My arms go around his neck, and he lifts me up until my legs are wrapped around his waist, kissing me like it's the end of the world. His tongue is sliding against mine, and I can feel his erection pressed against me, an answering ache echoing through my core. I grind against him, reaching to tear open his shirt.

He pulls back. "Not here," he growls, already walking me to the door. "You belong in *our* bed."

He carries me down the hallway to the primary bedroom, and the next thing I know, we're tumbling on the bed. Lifting up onto his knees on the mattress, he shrugs out of his suit jacket, and I sit up to rip his shirt open, making buttons fly everywhere. My palms run over his tattooed chest, and his hand fists my blonde hair, pulling until my head is tilted back. He presses open-mouthed kisses along the column of my throat until I'm moaning, dizzy in his arms.

I'm burning for him, impatient and needy.

"I know, Princess," he groans against me. "Fuck, I need you so bad."

Nero's mouth captures mine again, and he releases my hair to pull the top of my dress down. The material is stretchy, so it comes down my shoulders easily, and my chest is exposed. My bra disappears next, Nero unhooking it with an expert touch.

"Look at you..." he breathes, lifting his head long enough to drink in the sight of me, splayed on the covers. "Goddamn, you're a work of art."

He leans down to taste me, his lips moving across my chest, nipping my collarbone and licking along the swell of my breasts. My nipples become tight, and he captures one, flicking it with his tongue as I writhe, grinding against his erection.

God, we've barely started, and I'm already lost in a haze of pleasure.

"Patience, baby," Nero chuckles, toying with my nipple as I pant. "I'm taking my time tonight."

"But I need you," I hear myself whine, my voice high-pitched and desperate.

"You think I don't know exactly what you need?" Nero plants a hand on my chest and firmly pushes me back down, pinning me in place, and making my stomach leap with anticipation. "I know everything about this body... What makes you moan. What makes you scream. And you'll get it all, tonight. You can count on that."

And with that delicious promise, Nero returns to his mission, moving from one breast to the other, taking his time lavishing them with attention as his hips slowly gyrate, pressing his erection in just the right spot over and over again. God, he feels so good. I'm panting and moaning, shameless as I let him do whatever he wants to me.

Because he's right. Nobody knows my body like him.

Nobody can bring me a pleasure like this.

He pulls my dress off, mouth moving over my bare skin, worshiping every inch of me, moving lower.

And lower.

By the time he slides a finger under the lace of my panties, every muscle in my body is screaming for more.

"Tell me what you want," he murmurs softly.

He's taking off my panties so slowly, an inch at a time, and I can feel his warm breath blow on my core as it's exposed to him. I shudder.

"Nero..." I gasp.

"Tell me." This time, the words are an order. Thrilling me.

"I want you," I whisper, flushing. As if he can't see it for himself, I'm so wet for him.

"That's not good enough," he says, and I see amusement in his eyes. "Tell me exactly what you want me to do to you."

I shiver in delight. "I... I..." *Oh, to hell with it.* "I want you to taste me," I blurt in a breathless rush. "I want to feel your hands on my body, and your tongue... on me. I want you to hold me down and fuck me until you can't hold back, Nero. I want all of you."

My words come out in a desperate rush, but I know what I want, and I'm tired of denying myself.

Denying how perfect we are in these moments, lost to pure desire.

"That's my perfect, dirty Princess," Nero growls in approval, yanking my thighs wider apart. "Fuck, this pussy is so juicy," he says, running his thumb lightly over my clit. "I've been waiting all night to lick it clean."

He spits, right onto my tight bud, and I've barely gasped in shock at the crude gesture, before he's lowered his mouth to me, and is licking it up. Licking all of me, devouring my clit and spearing his tongue inside my drenched cunt.

"Oh God!" I cry out, clutching the bed sheets as pleasure slams through me.

"No, baby," Nero pauses, his eyes wild. "Don't pray to your God, he's not the one making this pussy go off. Pray to your *husband.*"

He shoves me back down and gets to work making me scream. *Fuck.* He's relentless, incredible. Lapping at me, sucking at the tender nub, until I give him what he wants.

His name, screamed so loud that all the neighbors can hear. "Nero!"

I come in a convulsion of pleasure, arching up, grabbing for him. But Nero flips my body over so I'm facedown on the mattress, yanking my hips up, so I'm positioned on all fours.

He slams forward, driving himself inside of me with a hard

thrust while I'm still climaxing.

Yes.

It's exactly what I need from him, and he knows it. Hard and thick inside me, mercilessly driving deep, filling me up to the brim.

"Fuck, yes," he groans. "Hot and tight. Lily, you're all *mine.*"

I rock back into him, groaning. He lands a spank on my already tender ass, and I moan even louder at the mingling of pleasure and pain.

Everything about being with Nero is a fiery contradiction. I tell myself that I shouldn't want it like this, but I do. I try to talk myself out of caring about him, but I can't.

I know it's wrong to need him, but fuck, it feels so right.

"That's right, baby," Nero grips my hips, slamming into me, setting a delicious rhythm. He grabs my hair in one hand, riding me, moving my body like I'm his to control.

Because I am.

I move with him, already feeling another crest building. "Nero!" I chant, gasping over and over. "Fuck, don't stop. Nero!" My screams echo, but I don't care. I don't care about anything right now except the driving force of Nero's cock, taking me to the precipice of pleasure.

And then I shatter with a cry, my orgasm claiming me so hard, my limbs give way, and I go limp. But Nero holds me up, fucking me through it. His thrusts get wild, an animal frenzy rutting into me.

"Fuck, Lily. *Fuck!*"

He comes with a roar, , pulling me up so that my back is pressed against his chest, grinding his cock up inside me. His mouth finds mine in a desperate kiss, binding us, mad with pleasure.

Together, no matter what.

Chapter 8

Lily

I wake up in Nero's bed—*our bed*—the sun shining through the open drapes and pooling, warm on my bare skin. I yawn, hazy with sleep, and the bone-deep pleasure of the night before.

"Morning, Princess."

I turn. Nero is watching me, head propped up on one hand. He reaches over and brushes hair from my eyes, dropping a soft kiss on my mouth.

I shiver with emotion, last night rushing back to me. Not just the mind-blowing sex, but how Nero held me, tight in his arms, until I fell asleep, feeling safe.

Loved.

"Morning," I whisper back. There's a rare tenderness in his eyes. I've seen it before, but not for a while now. Not with all the fighting and danger consuming our emotions.

It makes hope flicker to life, somewhere deep inside me.

"How did you sleep?" he asks, pulling me closer.

I stretch my arms over my head and arch my back, smiling. "Like I just ran a marathon."

He grins. "I should apologize... But I won't."

I nestle against him, head resting on his chest. I can feel his breathing, the steady rise and fall as he strokes slow circles on my naked back. It's soothing, the steady weight of him, protecting me, and I can't help wishing we could stay in this sunlit, morning bubble forever.

Nero must be reading my mind, or maybe he's been thinking the same thing, because he tilts my face up to look at him.

"Listen, I've been thinking..." he says, "Instead of you going right back to hating me, how about we take a timeout?"

I sit up. "A timeout?" I ask.

"Yeah, no fighting or drama or mafia shit," Nero says with a wry grin. "Just you and me, having a normal day, instead."

I smile a little and decide to play along. "You mean, pretend we're someone else? Like we're... George and Mary from Ohio?" I say, plucking names at random.

Nero chuckles, bringing my hand to his lips for a kiss. "Why not? We're just a boring couple from Cincinnati. I'm an accountant and you're a..."

"Librarian, of course," I add, enjoying this game. "I live a safe life among the books. And we live in a suburb, with an HOA and a perfectly green lawn."

"Well, it has to be." Nero teases. "The ladies from your book club would talk if I didn't take proper care of the grass."

"We wouldn't want that," I laugh, stretching against him. "And you could go fishing or play golf with the boys on the weekends. Oh, and I'm a member of the PTA, and I always sign you up for volunteer jobs at the school parties and fund raisers, which drives you crazy."

Nero's smile is bigger than I've seen it in a long time. "You're good at this game."

I pause. "I used to play it, just on my own. Imagine what life could be like... If my circumstances were different," I admit.

I see guilt flash in Nero's eyes. "But usually I'm off having fabulous international adventures," I add lightly, not wanting to wreck the mood. "George and Mary are a whole new ballgame."

Nero smiles again. "So, what do you say?" he asks. "Can we leave everything else behind, just for one day?"

There's something in the way he asks that makes me think he really needs this. He's showing me a side of himself that is rarely seen, an unguarded depth that he keeps hidden most of the time. It's enough to make my decision.

"Okay, *George*," I grin, kissing him lightly.

Nero's grip tightens, and I feel him swell, hard under my lap. I pretend to gasp. "But honey, this isn't our normal time for relations," I tease, wriggling on his stiff cock. "Whatever happened to once a week, before the nine o'clock news?"

"I'm being spontaneous, *Mary*," he replies. Then he climbs out of bed and scoops me up, pulling me into the bathroom as I laugh. Nero turns on the shower, and backs me straight under the warm spray, the both of us still naked.

"George," I scold playfully, even as his hands glide over me, making me moan. "Whatever will the neighbors say?"

"They'll say that's one lucky librarian," he grins, but his laughter turns to a low groan as I close my hand around his thick cock and begin to stroke.

"*Fuck*, baby..."

"Language, please," I giggle, feeling so free—and loving it.

Our kiss breaks off as Nero pulls away, his head falling back against the tiled wall. The cords of muscle stand out in his neck and his face twists with pleasure, watching my hand work up and down his shaft.

Then I sink to my knees.

His groans turn to whispered pleas, hands tangling in my wet hair. I tease him, barely running my tongue over the thick head, whispering kisses up his shaft until he's trembling with tension beneath me.

"Suck it, baby." Nero's voice twists. "Swallow my cock."

"Hmm..." I tease him more, loving the power flaring in my bloodstream. He's a dominant man, a force to be reckoned with, but even though I'm the one on my knees, he's totally at my mercy.

"What's the magic word?" I ask, swirling my tongue around to lap up the drops of salty pre-cum.

"Now," he growls, grip flexing, pumping his hips towards my mouth.

"Nope."

I go back to soft licks, and Nero groans again. "Baby..."

I lift my head, gazing up at him under the shower spray, water running in rivulets over his taut muscle. He's magnificent. Fearsome.

Mine.

"Just say the word," I coo, watching him unravel. I caress over his thighs, gently squeezing his balls, and he breaks.

"Fuck, Lily, *please.*"

Nero doesn't beg, but he begs for me. At the sound of my victory, I lean in, taking his cock in my mouth, as deep as I can.

"Fuck!"

Nero roars in pleasure, thrusting by instinct and embedding himself even deeper in the back of my throat. I have to struggle not to gag, but I quickly accommodate him, swallowing him down, and loving every minute of it.

God, I feel possessed. Consumed. All that matters is the thick, invasive stretch of him as I bob, sucking and licking at him, finding a rhythm that makes him curse like a drunk sailor, slamming his palm against the wall.

I can't believe it, but I'm getting close to the edge too. I reach between my legs, finding my aching core, fingering myself and palming my clit as I suck him down, pleasure overwhelming me. He thrusts faster, deeper, his shouts turning unintelligible as I feel his cock leap in my mouth.

"Lily, baby, I'm gonna—"

I moan around him, rubbing my swollen clit in a frenzy as I lift off him and sit back on my heels. "Mark me," I demand, presenting my bare breasts. "I want to feel you dripping all over me."

Nero's eyes flash in surprise and lust. "Goddamn, baby. You can take it, every drop."

He grabs his cock, pumping once, twice, before he comes with a roar, unleashing a torrent of hot come all over my naked chest. I feel the liquid paint me, and the sensation is so thrilling, I climax with a cry, clenching around my fingers.

Nero sinks to the shower floor beside me. "Well, fuck," he says, looking spent.

"Not bad, George," I say, laughing.

"You too, Mary." He laughs too, pulling me in for a sweaty kiss. Then he looks me over, stroking my damp breasts, rubbing his seed into my skin. "Looks good on you."

"It's a good thing we're already in the shower," I say. "Because I'm going to need to get cleaned up."

After soaping me from head to toe—and delivering yet another orgasm—Nero leaves me in the shower and heads downstairs. I take my time rinsing off, happiness light in my chest.

It may be just a time-out from our regular lives, but I don't care. I'm going to treasure every moment of this 'normal' day.

Even if I know these orgasms are nothing like normal.

Stepping out of the shower, I wrap myself in a fluffy robe.

The smell of bacon is wafting from downstairs, and I can't resist, so I don't even bother dressing before heading down in search of the scent.

Nero's in the kitchen, wearing jeans—and nothing else. "Delicious," I comment, padding barefoot into the room.

He grins. "Coffee?"

"Yes, please."

He sets about pouring me a mug, fixing it just the way I like, with cream and sugar. There's a plate of bacon on the counter and he's scrambling up eggs in a pan; the toaster pops up two pieces of golden toast.

"Can I do anything?" I ask, taken aback by the show of domesticity. I haven't seen Nero lift a finger in the kitchen since I arrived, it's all been takeout and chef deliveries.

"Nope. Sit that cute ass down," he says, handing me the coffee.

"I'm not going to argue with that." I steal a piece of bacon on my way to the table, enjoying the view.

He brings over our plates a few minutes later, and I wait until he settles into his chair across from me before starting to eat. "This is good," I say, tasting the eggs.

"Don't sound so surprised," he laughs.

"Can you blame me?" I shoot back with a smile. "I didn't think you knew how to turn the oven on."

"I'm a man of many talents."

"Yes, you are," I purr.

We eat in companiable silence for a moment, and Nero goes to refill his plate. "How's Teddy doing?" he asks, and my head snaps up. But Nero's question is sincere, with no hint of threat.

It's a normal day, remember?

"He's good," I say slowly. "He made the dean's list last

week. Although, I don't know when he gets any studying done, he's turned into a real ladies' man."

"You must be proud of him." Nero smiles.

"I am. I always knew he was smart, and I'm so happy that he gets to do something with that intelligence."

"He'll have the life you want him to have."

That sounds like a promise, but I can't rely on that. There are too many unknown factors at this point, too many things that can go wrong in our lives. That makes me think of Lydia's appearance at the restaurant last night.

"Is it true, what you said?" I ask. "Will the FBI back off now?"

Nero sighs. "Maybe. Vance was their mole, so with him out of the picture, it gives us a temporary reprieve, at least. And if I can close this deal with the Kovacks, then I'll be getting out of the criminal game for good. With nothing but legit real estate business on our books, there'll be less for the Feds to chase."

"Is the development going well?" I ask. They broke ground on construction over a month ago, and I know that Nero has been closely tracking the progress.

Nero nods, looking pleased. "Valuations on the buildings have already gone through the roof, and they aren't even up yet. It's the whole reason I've been planning the shift. There'll be more than enough cash to go around. We won't need to look over our shoulders anymore."

I know he means 'we' as in the Barretti organization, but still, I feel a flicker of hope inside of me. If this works out, it could change everything.

Maybe our pretend scenario could become more real...

I head to art class, and Nero goes to the construction site to deal with business, but we make plans to meet this evening at the bar. I practically float through my day, still caught up in the bubble of closeness. I decide I'm not going to worry about what happens after this pretense is over, I'm just going to savor feeling happy for the first time in a long while.

I deserve that, after everything I've been through.

After a great day's work and some of my favorite classes, I head to the bar.

I expect to find Nero in his office, away from the action, but he's seated at the bar, studying some paperwork.

"Hey," I say, sliding onto a stool beside him.

"Hi..." Nero gives me a distracted kiss, still checking the papers.

Avery stops by, behind the bar. "Don't take it personally," Avery she says with a smirk. "He's got his serious business frowny face on."

"Hmm? What did you say?" Nero asks without looking up.

She grins. "See? What can I get you?" she asks.

"Umm, a glass of wine would be great, thanks."

"I'll get the good stuff out of the back," Avery replies. "These idiots can't tell their chardonnay from their sauvignon."

She strolls off, and I watch Nero frown at the rows of dense financial figures. "Everything OK?" I venture.

He looks up and gives an apologetic sigh. "Yeah. Well, nope. The quarterly reports came through, and they're not adding up right."

"I didn't realize your *organization* cared so much about bookkeeping," I tease, amused.

Nero gives a wry chuckle. "We have to. Don't you remember, they got Capone on tax avoidance? You can bet these books stay squeaky clean. At least, they usually do." He looks past me, and calls to Miles, who approaches.

"What's up, boss?" Miles asks. His tousled blonde hair and glasses make him look angelic—and nerdy.

"Do me a favor, and take a look at these," Nero says, passing Miles the paperwork. "And see what the bookkeeper has to say for himself. We're missing, like, a hundred k here. And that's just from the main account, I haven't even looked at some of the other reports just yet—"

"No need!" Miles says quickly. "He already called. The bank made a mistake with the deposits. Should all be straightened out, end of the week."

"OK, good," Nero nods. "You'll take care of it?"

"No problem." Miles flashes me a weak smile, "Hey Lily."

"You want a drink?" Nero asks, but Miles shakes his head rapidly.

"I gotta go," he mumbles, and hurries away.

"Is he okay?" I ask, watching him weave his way through the tables. "He seems stressed."

"He worries, so I don't have to," Nero replies. Then he slides his arms around me, drawing me closer. He gives me a long, slow kiss, and I can feel the tension leave his body. "Better," he murmurs, stubble rough against my cheek. "Much better."

"Long day, George?" I ask, picking up our earlier teasing.

He smiles, rubbing my back. "They're all long these days, Mary."

"Who are George and Mary?" Avery asks, returning with my drink.

Nero smiles. "No one you know. Just a couple of easygoing people whose idea of going wild is ordering dinner from a new restaurant and opening a bottle of wine after the kids go to sleep."

Avery raises her eyebrows. "If this is some kind of kinky roleplaying thing, I don't want to know."

I snort with laughter—and realize that it's been way too long since I just relaxed, and had some fun. This 'normal' day has been going so well, why not make it last a little longer? "You know what?" I say impulsively. "We should have a girls' night."

Avery's face lights up. "Yes!" she exclaims, and I realize, I've never seen her hanging out with any female friends, either. She's either here, at the bar, or consulting with Nero on some life-and-death mafia business. "That sounds great."

"Uh oh," Nero jokes. "This is going to be trouble."

"Just a few girls on the town," I say sweetly. "What kind of trouble could we find?"

Chapter 9

Lily

I'm probably a little overexcited about girls' night, but I can't help myself. It's been so long since I did something like this. I take my time doing my hair and makeup back at the house, and then launch into a full-on fashion show to pick my outfit.

"Okay, what do you think?" I ask, showing off my third dress to Nero, as he reclines on the bed. The first one was too dressy. The second one was short, low-cut, and skintight. Nero nixed that before I'd even stepped all the way out of the bathroom.

I wouldn't normally let him tell me what I can and can't wear, but I had to admit that it was a little too revealing for me to be completely comfortable wearing. And he looked damn sexy and possessive, swearing nobody but him was going to see me like that.

Now, I'm modelling a cute fit-and-flare dress in navy blue, with towering strappy sandals, and some gold jewelry.

"I love it," he nods, looking amused. "But you know," he stands and strolls over, sliding his hands over my body, "if you wanted to put that second dress back on and blow off this outing, I could definitely make it worth your while."

His hands go to my hips, but I duck away, laughing. "Save it, mister. I'm really looking forward to this. Do you know how long it's been since I just hung out with friends?" I add, fluffing up my hair. "Years. Actual years!"

Nero smiles. "I like seeing you like this, all excited."

"You see me excited all the time," I throw him a wink, and he chuckles.

"Have fun," he says. "And when you get back... Well, you'll definitely have fun." He pulls me into a hot kiss, making his intentions clear. I give a happy sigh. A night on the town, and then a night in Nero's capable, muscular arms?

Sounds pretty perfect to me.

I Uber over to a buzzy bar in Soho to meet the others. Avery has already found us a table on the packed patio, and Juliet waves me over, sitting with a woman I don't recognize. I called her on a whim, she's always been kind to me, and since her husband is Nero's half-brother, she understands a little of my crazy life now.

"This was a great idea, Lily!" Juliet beams, greeting me. "You have no idea how much I needed a night out. This is my friend, Mara," she adds, introducing the other woman. She's a friendly looking brunette, with cute, cropped hair and funky eyeliner. "She's a designer at Sterling Cross."

"Oh, that's amazing," I smile. "I love the work there. You'll have to show me some of your designs."

"Lily's an artist, too," Juliet announces, and I blush.

"Not really. I'm just taking some classes right now."

"Don't be modest," Juliet smirks. "Can you imagine a table of guys all sitting around, being self-deprecating?"

"'No, don't pay any attention, I'm really insignificant and boring,'" Avery plays along, mimicking in a low voice. We all laugh, and I know right away that tonight is going to be fun.

I look around and gesture the waitress over. "Who wants what?" I ask, ordering a margarita.

"Mojito, thanks," Mara says.

"Ooh, I'll get an espresso martini," Avery decides. "I can't get any girly drinks with the guys, they give me so much shit," she adds, rolling her eyes.

I laugh. "What about you, Juliet?"

She pauses. "Umm, just a lime and soda water, thanks."

The waitress leaves. "Not going to cut loose with the rest of us?" I ask Juliet, teasing.

"Not tonight."

I catch a flash of happiness in her expression. "Wait a minute..." I gasp. "Are you...?"

She beams wider, unable to keep the smile off her face. "Maybe..."

"Juliet!"

"Wait, what?" Avery looks over, confused.

I look to Juliet for confirmation, and she gives a little nod.

"Juliet's knocked up!" I announce.

Mara squeals so loudly, the people nearby turn to stare. "Mind your own business," Avery tells them, then joins in the congratulations.

"You have to keep it between us," Juliet hushes us. "It's early. We aren't announcing it yet."

"Still, this is amazing news," I tell her, feeling choked up. "We have to celebrate! And soda water just won't cut it. What have you been craving?" I demand, and she grins.

"Well, it's going to sound gross, but I've been going crazy for the pickled herring at Veselka."

"First of all, ewww," Avery says. "And second, also ewww."

I laugh, raising my glass in a toast. "Pickled herring, here we come!"

We drink a couple of rounds at the bar, catching up on gossip, and all the scoop from Sterling Cross' celebrity clients. Juliet is planning a big event for the company, a red carpet gala to launch their latest collection, and we all ooh and ahh over her pictures of the designs. Then we make our way to the East Village, and the old Ukrainian restaurant Juliet is loving. We order pierogis and goulash, crowding into a table by the window. Around midnight, Mara lets out a regretful yawn.

"Sorry, kids, I need to call it. We're driving to Ashville tomorrow to visit his parents."

"You mean, today?" I joke.

She groans. "I'll sleep in the passenger seat."

Mara says her goodbyes and heads out, leaving Juliet, Avery, and me alone. Avery flags down the scowling waitress. "Two vodka shots, thank you."

"More?" I groan. "I don't know about that. After this food, I'm ready for a nap."

"You'll learn, keeping up with Nero," she gives a wry grin.

"The great, invincible Nero Barretti," Juliet adds meaningfully. "I was going to say something. Even Caleb was shaken up, hearing the news."

I wince. "Sorry about that."

"It was quite the resurrection. Everything OK?" she asks.

It's no coincidence she waited until Mara left before turning the conversation to the highly shady activities of our lives.

"It's... As OK as things can get, living in his world," I reply. The vodka arrives, so I take a shot, feeling tipsy and more loose-lipped than usual. "He didn't tell me what was going on," I confide. "I thought he was dead, too. Until I walked in and saw that smug, annoyingly sexy face staring back at me."

"Oh wow." Juliet's eyes widen.

"Yup!"

Avery gives me a look. "Don't take it personally. Nero's used to calling all the shots."

"Yes, yes he is."

"Must run in the family," Juliet adds with a smirk. "I thought I'd got a handle on Caleb being overprotective, but this pregnancy is bringing out the caveman in him."

"They don't make it easy to love them," I muse.

"Yes, but it's good even when it's hard," Juliet replies.

Avery smirks. "That's what she said."

We all laugh. It's nice, knowing these women understand even a little of the world I'm in.

"What about you, Avery?" I ask curiously. "Are you dating?"

She snorts with laughter. "Yeah, no. You see any eligible bachelors hanging around the Barrettis, looking to sweep me off my feet?"

"I don't know, there are some cute ones," I play a hunch, meeting her eyes. "Miles, for example."

Avery chokes on her water, looking flustered. "What? No. I mean, maybe. I haven't noticed."

"You're blushing!" I crow.

"You have a crush," Juliet adds, singsong.

"And you two are being immature." Avery mops herself down and gives us a withering stare. We laugh, but Avery looks thoughtful.

"I don't know... I wonder, if it's even possible. Being in this world, wanting something like love..."

Juliet reaches out and squeezes her hand. "It'll work out if it's meant to. Things were pretty complicated between me and Caleb for a long time, but look at us now."

Her eyes meet mine, and I wonder if she's only saying it for Avery's benefit.

"How did you know?" I find myself asking. "How did you know it would be worth it, all the chaos and hurt?"

She pauses. "I guess I didn't. All I knew was that I loved him, enough to fight whatever came our way. Enough to fight for us. I'm glad I stuck it out through the crazy, because I really couldn't be happier now."

I feel an ache, a part of me desperately hoping that she's right. If I take a chance on Nero, if I follow my heart to him, could we have a chance at a happily-ever-after?

Could the drama all be worth it in the end?

* * *

I make it home a little after one, tipsy and smiling from our night of fun.

"Hello?" I call. The lights are on, but I don't see Nero anywhere, so I head to the kitchen, stripping off my jacket and kicking my shoes aside as I go. I walk over to the sink and turn on the faucet. I'm so thirsty, I don't even find a glass, I just duck my head and drink straight from the tap, splashing water all over me.

"Real classy, Lily," I tell myself, laughing.

"Are you talking to yourself?"

I spin around to see Nero standing there, watching me with a half-smile on his face. He's so handsome when he smiles, even a little one like this. I wish he'd do it more often.

"Do you see anyone else here?" I ask. "I mean, beside you. But your name's not Lily, is it?"

Now he chuckles. "No. No, it isn't."

He watches as I bend over and take another drink. The cool liquid feels great in my parched throat.

"Did you have fun?" Nero asks.

I grin. "I really did. It was low-key, and I didn't realize it, but that was exactly what I needed. And Avery is so funny! Did you know that?"

I head toward him. It's easier to walk now that my heels are off, and I don't stop until I'm pressed up against Nero, chest to chest.

"I did know that," he says, but I've already forgotten what I was talking about. I'm distracted by the look of desire in his eyes. He wants me. I'm probably a tipsy mess right now, but he wants me.

"Yes, I do."

"Did I say that out loud?" I giggle, and he nods. His smile is growing.

I run my hand down his chest, tracing the hard muscles beneath his black T-shirt. I thought about having him all to myself for so long during the years we were apart, and now that I can have him any time I want, I don't know why I'm not sleeping with him every damn night.

My intoxicated mind doesn't understand these sober decisions I've been making.

"Go take a seat," I tell him, pointing to the living room.

He grins. "You're drunk."

"Just a little," I wink. "So play your cards right, and you might get lucky."

He chuckles, following my direction to a chair in the living room. I push him back lightly, so he's sitting down. "What are you up to?"

"You'll see," I reply airily. "Google, play 'sexy playlist'."

Nero looks at me, still amused. "We don't have that tech in the house. Security, remember?"

"Oh, right!" I sashay over to my purse, and click to connect my phone to the speakers, scrolling until I find the music I want.

The low, sexy chords sound loudly, and I swing my hips, strolling back to him. It's a good thing I've had a few drinks, because I would never be so bold, but right now, I still feel invincible.

I want to have some fun.

"Like the view?" I ask, swaying closer, dancing to the music now. Nero's eyes follow my hands as I glide them over my body, stroking over my breasts and hips.

"Always," he replies. He reaches for me, but I lightly slap his hand away.

"No touching during the dance."

He sits back, smiling. "I didn't know there were rules."

"I'm in charge tonight. Just relax..."

I waited tables at strip clubs in Vegas for years, and I may not have been a performer, but you can be damn sure that I learned a few moves.

Leaning in, I slowly gyrate above him, my breasts just inches from his face. He exhales, gripping the chair arms. I smile. "That's right. I'm off-limits, baby. Nothing to do but watch."

I straighten, tugging the hem of my dress higher. Higher. Until I'm easing it over my head.

Nero's eyes darken with lust. I'm standing here in matching black panties and a bra, that barely qualify as either. I shimmy for him, turning a full circle, and slowly bending over to give him a view of my ass. I peek back. I can already see his erection, bulging in the lap of his pants.

Ready for me.

I turn back, dancing my way over, grinding now, up against him. My bra has a front clasp, so I unhook it, letting it pop open and expose my breasts. Nero's hands start to move to them, but I give him a look.

"You want me to stop?" I ask, warning.

He gives a tortured grin. "No."

"Thought not."

I go back to my dance, laying back over his lap as I run my hands over my bare skin. I'm grinding back against him, giving him a view right the way down to where I'm teasing over my panties, his breath hot in my ear.

"That's right, baby," Nero groans. "Touch it for me. Play with that pretty pussy."

I ease my hand under the silk, teasing. I can tell that he's enjoying this little show. I can feel it pressing into my ass and see it in his dark expression. He looks *hungry*.

I slide my fingers through the slickness and give a moan.

Nero groans in answer. "How does it feel?" he asks hotly. "Tell me."

"So wet," I moan again, flexing my fingers. "So tight, and ready for you."

He's still gripping the chair arms, but he thrusts up, grinding his thick erection into my ass as I gyrate. "Fuck, Lily. I don't how much more of this I can take."

"You'll take whatever I give you," I coo. I push my panties down completely and spread my legs on either side of his. Sitting on his lap now, my back to his chest. Lying against him, touching myself for him to see.

"Fuck." His breathing is ragged in my ear, and I feel his body tight with tension. "Look at you, baby. You're getting close, I can tell. Your nipples are begging for a lick, aren't they?" he groans. "So tight, baby. You need my tongue to help you out. Get you off, real good?"

I moan, tempted. But I'm loving this control he's given me, and I'm going to make the most of it.

I twist in his lap, so I'm straddling him, face-to-face.

"Take it off," I tell him, nodding to his shirt. He does it immediately. "Pants too."

These require my help, but soon, he's naked beneath me. I take a moment to appreciate his sculpted body, the thick muscle and dark ink of his tattoos.

Again, I feel that possessive urge. *All mine.*

Nero's hands move to my hips. I shake my head. "Rules still apply," I remind him, moving them back to the chair arms. "And right now... You're at my mercy. What will I do with you?" I muse.

Kissing his lips, I rake my nails lightly down his chest and abs, stopping before I reach his cock. He pushed his tongue into my mouth, unable to resist the urge to do something to dominate a part of me. I let him for a moment before pulling away.

My mouth goes to his chest. I flick my tongue over one nipple, then the other one as my hand wraps around his erection. I start to stroke him, but slowly. I don't want him anywhere near coming until he's inside of me.

"God, baby..." Nero's head sinks back with a groan.

I smile, remembering his filthy words to me the other night. "Don't pray to your god," I echo, sultry. "Pray to your *wife*."

Nero's eyes meet mine, and a moment of electric connection passes between us. Because it's the first time I've called myself that and meant it.

I swallow hard, unprepared for the rush of emotion, so I focus back on my sexy teasing instead. I keep stroking his cock, until Nero starts to pant.

"You're driving me crazy," he groans, but he's not really complaining. We both know there's pleasure in this kind of torment, that anticipation can take all of this to a whole new level.

"You drive me crazy—every damn day," I point out, cooing

in his ear. I'm straddling his lap, fisting his cock between us, the damp tip nestled between my thighs. "You walk in the room, and I'm wet for you. Aching. It's only fair I get to return the favor."

I'd never say these things if I was sober, but right now, I couldn't feel more free. Power is throbbing in my veins, and fuck, desire is taking over, too.

Positioning myself above his lap, I slowly sink down, taking his cock all the way to the hilt.

"Lily!" He gives a ragged cry, and I answer it with my own desperate moan.

Fuck, he feels so good.

"You feel that?" I ask, flexing and clenching around him. "You feel how much I need you?"

"Yes," Nero curses, thrusting up inside me. "Fuck, yes!"

My hands settle on his chest, and I start to ride him, grinding his cock as I keep my eyes on him. It's slow and dirty and intimate, him watching me like this, taking my pleasure, rising up and sinking down, moaning with every thick stretch and stroke.

"That's it, baby," he urges me on, gasping. "Take it, Princess. Take all of it. Ride my dick like you own it. Every fucking inch, baby, it's all for you."

I do it.

I take what I need, moving faster, until I'm bouncing up and down on him with wild abandon. Pleasure climbing, my breasts swaying, our bodies making a slick noise in the dim light. "Yes," I'm moaning, "Nero, God, yes!"

His control finally breaks. He grabs me around the waist and rears up, slamming me down as he thrusts, impaling me on his cock.

I scream in pleasure, mindless. I'm so close to the edge and Nero is right there with me, incoherent grunts of pleasure coming from his mouth. He finds my lips, and kisses me deeply, drinking me in as our bodies thrust and grind. It's perfect, a pleasure beyond belief. My orgasm crests, and then breaks through me like a tidal wave, sweeping over every part of me as I toss my head back and howl.

"Nero!"

He thrusts up again, grinding me against him, friction driving against my sensitive bud as his cock possesses me, sending fresh shockwaves through my body, over and over again as he comes with a roar, gripping me so tightly, I know there'll be marks in the morning.

I don't mind. He's already left an indelible mark, on the only place that matters.

On my heart.

Chapter 10

Nero

I wake up in a hell of a good mood. It doesn't matter that there are nail marks scratching up my chest from Lily's wildcat routine last night. The sting is more than worth it.

And fuck, anything would be worth the show she gave me. The sight of her tits bouncing for me, that wicked glint in her eye as she writhed on my lap, fingers in her cunt...

I'll take that memory to the grave, alright.

I roll over. She's still asleep next to me, snuggling close and naked in the sheets. I can't resist spooning her, the peach of her ass rubbing up against my morning erection. *Damn.* I stroke her naked skin and seriously consider waking her for another round, but I have business demanding my attention today, and if I start it off by sinking into her tight warmth, I won't ever want to leave.

Regretfully, I pull away, just as she starts to stir. I slide out of bed, smiling at the way she opens her eyes and flinches from the light. She's too fucking adorable hungover, just like she was, tipsy and excited last night.

She groans. "Too bright," she mumbles, burying her face in the pillows.

"That's the vodka talking," I say, stroking back her hair. "You need some hair of the dog, that's all."

"Like hell," she mumbles without even opening her eyes. "I'm never drinking again."

Yeah, right.

Hell, I'll encourage her to go out drinking with the girls more often if it always ends in the kind of kinky sex we had last night.

I hop in the shower, then dress and head downstairs to grab fresh glass of water for her. I set the water on the nightstand along with a bottle of aspirin.

"I'm heading out," I say softly, but she's already asleep again, so I press a gentle kiss to her forehead, shut the drapes, and leave her to sleep it off in the dark room. She looks so angelic, splayed there across the pillows, I would never have guessed the way she took control, driving me to the edge of oblivion with her sultry temptation. And the way she rode me, demanding everything I had to give with that tight pussy sliding down my cock...

Yeah, my wife has hidden depths, alright.

I leave her a quick note, telling her to meet me at the new construction site later. The development is coming along well, and I want to show her the progress. She's the reason it's even moving ahead, but as I get in the car and head out, I try to put our night of passion out of my mind and focus on business.

Where I'm heading, I can't risk any distraction, or hint of affection.

Today, I'm visiting my father.

He summoned me to come visit, and I'm tense as I drive upstate and arrive at the prison. I go through security and wait in the private visiting room, wondering what's on his mind today. I'm guessing that it's not good. Although he's been locked up for ten years now, and I've been in control of the organization, I know he still doesn't approve of the way I run things.

Tough shit.

I brace myself as he walks into the room. Time has taken its toll, and he's a long way from the towering mob boss I remember from my childhood: gray-haired and limping slightly as he takes a seat at the table, brow furrowed in a disapproving scowl.

"You keeping well?" I ask, keeping my voice even.

"Well enough." He regards me stonily. "Better than you, at least. Heard you went and got yourself killed."

And I'm sure you were just heartbroken.

I give a casual shrug. "You know how it is. Sometimes you've got to go to extremes to smoke out a rat."

"And you're sure it was Vance?" Roman narrows his eyes, and it's no surprise why. He's the one who sent Vance to keep tabs on me. 'Protection', he called it.

Some protection that traitor turned out to be.

In fact...

Staring at my father, I have to wonder. Was any of this *his* doing?

"You need to pick your men more carefully," I tell him, keeping my suspicions to myself. I'm his only son. He wouldn't hurt me.

Would he?

I shake it off. "Vance was a rat, *and* he tried to kill me. That doesn't say much about his loyalty to you."

Roman sighs. "It's hard to find good help these days."

I narrow my eyes. "Is that the only reason I'm here? Wanted to make sure your little boy was alive and kicking?"

Roman fixes me with a glare. "I've heard things.

Worrying things. I want to believe my source is wrong, but there are people saying that you've been talking with the Kovacks."

Damn.

I hide my reaction, as icy as my father. A mirror of his poker face. "Like you said, good help is hard to find. Someone's been spinning you bullshit."

"Is it true?" he demands.

"What benefit would there be to speaking with them?" I say vaguely.

He scowls. "In case you get ideas, we don't do things that way. There's them and us. No common ground. That's how it's always been. It's how we keep a stronghold on the city."

"Times change," I can't resist saying. "You ever think we'll be left in the dust? One of these days, we'll need to think about what comes next. Getting out of this game."

Roman's eyes narrow. "Over my dead body," he growls. "This is no game, it's my fucking legacy. And you need to uphold that, or…" he pauses, meeting my eyes in a cool stare.

"Or what?"

"Or I'll find someone who will."

* * *

My father's threat echoes all the way back to the city.

Is he serious? I don't know, but I do know that you don't underestimate Roman fucking Barretti.

Not unless you want to end up with a bullet in the back of your skull.

I think about Vance, and his confused actions. Shopping me to the Feds is one thing—maybe they caught him in a bad rap, and he decided to sell me out, or even just take the cash. But trying to kill me?

That's a whole different game plan. Clearing the decks at the top of the organization.

Moving power back to my father...

I'm still thinking about it when I stop by the bar and find Chase waiting in my office.

"All good at lockup?" he asks, taking a seat.

I nod. "The usual Roman bullshit, you know how it is."

And he does. Chase has been my brother-in-arms since we were kids. He knows my father's tricks better than anyone.

"The old man's a stubborn bastard, but he knows a few things," Chase offers. "Maybe he has some perspective on this Kovack situation. I still think they set us up with the Feds. We gotta send a message, make it clear the Barrettis won't take their shit."

I sigh. There's a reason I invited Chase here, and he's not going to like it.

" I need to fill you in on a few things." I start. "Shit's changing around here, and it's time you knew about it."

"What kind of changes?" Chase's expression shifts, wary.

I pour him a drink. "I've been in talks with Igor and Sergei."

"What the fuck?" Chase pushes the glass I offer away, spilling booze on the floor. He leaps to his feet, but I stand my ground, eye-to-eye. Chase is my closest friend, but if he attacked me, I'd put him in the ground. I won't be disrespected in that way.

"Sit." I say it quietly, but there's no mistaking the steel in my voice.

He stares me down a moment, but finally slumps back into the seat.

"We've come to an agreement," I continue. "An easing of hostilities between us. They're going to start buying out our operations in the city, until we're out of the game for good."

Chase shakes his head, looking disgusted. "Are you out of your fucking mind? That's Barretti territory, and you're just giving it up? Land we've fought and bled for. That our men have died for."

"I'm not giving it up, I'm selling it for a premium, I might add. And those men are the reason I'm doing this," I shoot back. "What other solution do you see? More blood spilled, more good men dying, and for what?"

"For honor," Chase grinds out. "For power."

"We can have power without all this bullshit carnage." I insist. "Hell, the cash coming in from this real estate development will dwarf anything the Barrettis have ever made from crime. We'll be able to buy this whole city. That's real power—and it doesn't mean sacrificing our futures, either."

"*Future?*" Chase makes a contemptuous snort. "Yeah, I should have guessed. This is about Lily, isn't it?"

He's scornful, and I feel my defenses raise at the mention of her name.

"This plan was in motion long before she came back into my life," I inform him coldly. "Hell, I've mentioned it often enough."

"And I hoped you'd see sense," he replies. "Realize this is as good as it gets. Fuck, Nero, you're giving up, when you should be doing the opposite. *Expanding* Barretti territory, not shrinking it. Run this city, the way your father always dreamed." He urges me. "It's your destiny. It's in your fucking blood."

His words are a familiar refrain. I've been hearing them my whole goddamn life. And I always believed them, too.

Until Lily made me want something different.

Made me believe I could take it.

"My destiny is what I make it," I tell him fiercely. "And I'm not asking permission, I'm telling you, this is how it's going down. Get with the program or get the fuck out."

Chase gets up again, shoving his chair aside. "This is bullshit," he scowls. "You'll see."

He turns away from me and storms out of the office.

I sigh. That went about as well as I expected, but still, I hate that he sees my moves as a betrayal, instead of the ultimate sign of loyalty.

It's because I care about my people that I want them to be safe. Able to live their lives without the constant threat of violence and death.

Able to build a future, without wondering if tomorrow will come.

But he's right, too. Even though my plans were in motion long before Lily came back into my life, having her here has made me even more certain that this is the right path. As much as we joke about George and Mary, and their ordinary suburban lives, I can see the longing in her eyes, thinking about a normal life.

No Feds, or rival gangs. No explosions, or constant threat of danger.

I want to give that to her. Hell, I want it for myself. To wake up with her every morning like I did today and know that I can keep her safe. To build a future together. A home.

Having kids who won't grow up the way I did: Cursed to continue my father's twisted legacy.

And now, it's finally within reach.

I finish up at the office, and head over to the construction site. I've spent years strategically buying up buildings in one neighborhood on the east side of Manhattan, buying out tenants and bribing landlords with whatever cash it took. Now, I have a parcel of land that stretches an entire city block. With Lily's help, and my take-no-prisoners tactics, I secured all the zoning permits I needed to raze it to the ground, and start transforming the rundown buildings into a huge, high-end developments. Retail. Offices. Luxury condos. This isn't small-time mafia shit, this is the next level. Billionaire territory. The value is already skyrocketing, and I've had numerous offers to buy, for ten times what I've put in.

I turned them all down. *This* is going to be the new Barretti legacy. A billion-dollar empire, totally legal and legit.

And all mine.

I drive onto the site, which is the usual madhouse of construction, crew, and equipment. The skeleton of one of the first buildings is up, towering ten stories high—and climbing. I find Kyle hanging out with the town car, so I pull up beside him, and get out.

"Lily around?" I ask.

"She's around here... Somewhere. She wanted to see the place."

I pull out my phone, and call. "You beat me to it," I tell her. "I wanted to give you the tour."

She giggles. I can hear from the background noise, she's somewhere nearby. "You know me, I don't like to wait. Look up."

"Where?" I shield my eyes against the sinking sun.

"The elevator."

I turn, spotting her. One of the rudimentary construction elevators is slowly hoisting up the building, and Lily's standing on it behind the safety barrier, along with my foreman. "You said the view will be the best in the city," she continues, waving down at me. "I wanted to take a peek. You know, maybe we should live in one of these condos. Penthouse, obviously."

I laugh. "Sure you can afford it?"

I'm teasing her, but the truth is that I like that she's thinking about a future that includes me.

"No, but I have a very generous husband." Lily says. "And if I play my cards right, he'll—"

Her words cut off by a grinding noise.

"What's that?" I ask, feeling a chill.

"I don't know. Nero—"

Her answer cuts off with a chilling scream, as before my eyes, one of the elevator cables snaps, and the entire rig goes plummeting toward the ground.

Chapter 11

Lily

I'm in a nightmare. The elevator falling so fast, weightless, and all I can do is grip the side railing and scream.

Beside me, the site foreman is holding on for dear life too, and the terror on his face makes me panic even more.

He thinks we're going to die.

Oh God. My stomach is in my throat. The elevator is whistling towards the ground like a speeding bullet, and fear makes my heart pound wildly against my ribcage.

This can't be the end.

I haven't even started loving him yet.

As soon as that thought crosses my mind, something grinds into place and the elevator jerks to a halt. The motion is so violent, we slam into the floor. I land hard on my shoulder and hip as the breath is knocked out of my lungs, as the elevator platform swings wildly.

Just fifteen feet above the ground.

I peer over the edge, reeling. Just a couple more seconds, and we would have smashed into the concrete.

Just a couple more seconds, and I would be dead.

"Get that damn thing down!"

I hear Nero's yell, and relief floods me. Seconds later, the elevator makes its jerky descent, the final few feet.

I stumble out, desperate to get away from the thing. I fall into Nero's arms, shaking.

"Are you OK?" he demands, eyes wild with panic. "Lily, talk to me!"

"I... I'm OK," I manage, clinging onto him. He holds me close. I feel something trickle down my forehead and swipe at it, only to come away with blood on my hand. I wince when I find a cut near my hairline. It must have happened when I was slammed into the floor of the elevator.

"Someone find out what the hell happened," he barks out, not releasing me. "Andy, you good?"

"I'll live," the foreman replies, looking just as shaken up.

"I want a full safety check, every damn rig in this place," Nero demands furiously. "And for fuck's sake, don't let anyone else near those things."

The men go to work checking out the elevator while Nero leads me away from the construction. I pull large gasps of air into my lungs. I'm so freaked out that I feel lightheaded, my legs numb.

"Here, sit," he places me on a stack of lumber, holding my face gently in his hands as he turns my head one way and then another. "Did you hit your head? Are you dizzy?"

I swallow, shaking. "I... don't know."

"Fuck, Lily..." Nero trails off, looking grim. "I thought..."

"Me too." I focus on my breathing, and holding Nero tightly, and slowly, I begin to feel more stable again.

One of the construction workers approaches. "Boss?" he asks, looking nervous.

"What is it?" Nero snaps, his gaze never leaving me.

"I, uh, checked the elevator. The main cable failed. Luckily, the safety backup kicked in time."

"The cable failed?" Nero's head snaps up. "How does that happen?"

The poor guy coughs. "It, uh, looks like it was cut."

As I'm processing it, the foreman joins us, looking more collected. "This wasn't an accident," he confirms, showing Nero a picture on his phone. "If it had frayed naturally, there'd be ragged fibers. But look, sliced clean through."

"Sabotage."

Nero looks down at me, and I can see the shock in his expression. Then his eyes harden, hiding any trace of emotion. "Fix the elevator," he says curtly. "Post security, and comb every inch of this fucking site for more signs of tampering. I don't care how long it takes; I want this place locked down. Understand?"

"Got it, boss."

Nero leads me to the car where Kyle is waiting, looking pale as his eyes meet mine. I guess he caught the show, too. But I don't have it in me to reassure him that I'm fine. I just get in the back of the car when Nero holds the door open for me.

"Take us home."

I sink back in the cool leather seats, worn out. "Who could have done this?" I ask, turning to Nero. Now that the initial shock is fading, my head is buzzing with questions.

He shakes his head grimly. "I don't know."

"But I don't understand. Were they trying to hurt you? Or one of the crew—?

My words are cut short by Nero placing his finger to my lips.

"I don't have answers yet, but don't worry. I'll get them. Just relax, baby. It's over. Everything's going to be OK."

He puts his arm around me, drawing me close, and I sink

into his embrace. Needing the security, as my body still hums with adrenaline and fear for the whole ride home.

When we pull up outside our house, Nero insists on carrying me inside.

"I'm fine," I protest, as he places me gently on the couch.

"You don't look fine."

He strides to the kitchen, and runs the cold faucet on a cloth, returning to dab at the blood on my forehead. I wince, and his eyes darken. "Where else do you hurt?"

"Everywhere?" I admit. My entire body is bruised and sore.

"I'll call the doctor to come check you out."

"No." I shake my head. "I don't want to deal with being poked and prodded and asked a million questions right now. Please?"

Nero doesn't look happy. "Fine, but I'm going to clean this cut on your forehead and check out the rest of you," he insists. "If I think you're seriously hurt, the doctor is coming."

I nod, relieved, and sink back into the cushions as he fetches a first aid kit, and carefully tends to my wound. It stopped bleeding in the car, and it doesn't hurt unless I touch it, so I have a feeling the cut isn't deep. Nero's unhurried, taking extra time to be gentle as he applies anti-bacterial cream and a bandage, fingertips light on my skin.

There's something intimate about this, but not in a sexual way. His face is close to mine, our breathing in sync. I'm comforted by his nearness, and I slowly exhale the last of the tension gripping me—until the front door flies open, and Chase charges in.

Nero straightens. "What's the situation?" he barks, all business again.

Chase looks pissed. "It was them. The Kovacks."

Nero tenses. "Impossible."

"I talked to the guys at the site," Chase insists. "They saw a guy hanging around the last couple of days. Spoke with a Russian accent, serpent tattoo on his right arm. Sound familiar, yet?"

Nero swears. "Igor gave me his word."

"And I warned you, their word means nothing." Chase's eyes flit to me briefly, "Guess they were planning something for you, but couldn't pass up the chance to send a message with *her.*"

Chase's words send a shiver of fear down my spine. I hate the idea that my entire existence is being reduced to my relationship with Nero. It's as if I'm not even a person, just a means to an end.

Nero paces, and I can tell, he's trying to process this. "We need more information," he says. "Have you pulled the security footage?"

"Didn't you hear me?" Chase exclaims. "They've come after you. They tried to kill your wife. The détente is dead. It's over. We need to go to war!"

"No!"

Nero's voice rings out. Chase freezes.

"We're not starting a war that will bring carnage to our streets, not on a fucking whim," Nero continues. "Don't get me wrong, I want to tear apart the son of a bitch who's responsible, but we're going to be fucking smart about this. Nobody makes a move tonight. You understand?"

Chase scowls.

"Do. You. Understand. Me?" Nero grinds out the words.

Chase shakes his head in clear disgust. "Fine. You stay here and fuck around with the little wifey while we're made to look like fools. I'm gonna go get a drink."

Chase leaves the way he came in, angry. The door slams behind him.

I look to Nero. "Do you think that's true? Are the Kovacks behind this?"

He's still pacing. "I don't know."

"You had a deal."

He nods. "Question is, is this Igor breaking his word, or one of his guys going rogue? And does it even matter?" he asks, as if asking himself. "If I can't trust him to keep his men in line..."

He turns back to me. "I hate that they hurt you. That you're in danger every fucking time you walk out that door."

"But I'm fine," I insist again.

"This time."

"This time is all that matters," I lie, knowing it's not exactly true, but needing him to relax a moment. I don't want to lose him to the darkness in his frown, so I take his hand, pressing it to my lips in a kiss. "Every time they come for us, we make it," I remind him. "And they can keep trying. We'll beat them again, whatever it takes."

Nero sighs.

"I need to lay down," I tell him. "Take me to bed?"

He nods, and helps me up the stairs to our bedroom. But I don't let him go. I pull him towards the bed with me.

"Stay," I whisper, stripping off my shirt.

"You need to rest," Nero says, but he doesn't go anywhere.

I shuck off my pants, too. "I said, I wanted to lay down," I correct him, taking his hand and moving it to my bare body. "With you."

"Baby..." he leans closer, kissing me. "I don't want to hurt you."

"You won't. I want you, Nero," I swallow hard. "Make me forget it all. Please?"

I need this right now. I need the comfort of his touch, to feel a connection that confirms I'm alive and well. I need to be with Nero because I almost lost everything.

And maybe he feels the same, because he nods, laying me gently down onto the bed. He strips out of his own clothing while I watch, his erection springing free. Coming down onto the bed, he settles beside me, stroking softly over my body. I gasp, moving closer. Touching him, too. If our sex was frenzied last night, today, it's something else. Something sweeter. He takes his time lavishing my breasts with his tongue, his hands caressing my skin. He's still in charge, teasing out my pleasure as he switches his move to my other breast, his teeth grazing the sensitive bud, but there's something about the way his eyes keep flicking up to my face and the unhurried way that he's touching and tasting parts of my body.

It's almost as if he's savoring the moment. Or cherishing it.

Finally, his hands move to my panties, stroking me through the silk. I moan, pressing against his hand as I fist his cock in mine. Our eyes meet as we touch each other, drawing gasps and groans. I pump him slowly, as his fingers rub my clit in hypnotic circles. Pressure rising. *Connected.*

"Please..." I whisper, finally writhing with impatience. "I need you inside me."

Nero brushes hair from my eyes. "Say it again," he urges, "God, I love to hear you say it."

"I need you," I moan again. "I need your cock deep inside me, and the weight of you pinning me down. There's nothing like it in the world."

"My Lily..." Nero rolls above me, and parts my thighs. "I need you too, baby. More than air. Fuck, the feel of this sweet cunt..."

He sinks into me slowly, and I arch up, loving the thick stretch of it.

"Yes," I moan. "*More.*"

He thrusts inside of me, swallowing my moan as he presses his lips to mine once again. I hold onto him as he starts to work his way in and out of me, riding me slow but deep. Taking his time to find the perfect angle, the one that makes me shake and clutch at him.

"Oh *God*," I thrust back, trying to speed our pace, but Nero won't be hurried.

He holds me down and fucks me slowly, until I can't take it anymore.

"Nero!" my voice rises, pleasure coursing through my veins. "I'm close. God, don't stop."

"Never," he vows. "I'll never stop pleasing you."

Never...

I shiver, grief suddenly mingling with pleasure in a swell of emotion. I could have died today. I almost did.

What would the last thing I said to Teddy have been? Would Avery know how much her friendship meant to me? Did Nero have any idea that I felt so much more than anger toward him?

I don't know the answers to these questions, so I hold on tighter to Nero, allowing the pleasure he's giving me to wash away those concerns. This is why I need him so much. I want to lose myself in the way that only he can make happen.

"*Yes*, Nero... It's so good... So good..." I feel almost delirious as I'm driven closer to ecstasy. It's just out of my reach, but I know I'll get there.

He always gets me there.

"I've got you," Nero murmurs, thrusting slowly. Angling his cock just right to stroke my inner walls and send me wild. "Let go for me, baby. *Come*,"

With those words, he reaches a hand between us and expertly finds my clit with his thumb. Stroking me—in time with his thrusts, driving me to the edge—and beyond.

Yes!

Every part of my body tightens, and I feel a rush of pleasure that completely overwhelms me. I clutch him, crying out in bliss, and he sounds a groan of pleasure, thrusting into me again and staying there, embedded inside me, unleashing his own climax as we ride this wave together.

I collapse back, gasping. Tiredness overwhelms me, and I turn into Nero, nuzzling my face into the crook of his neck. I relax, safe in the steely embrace of his arms wrapped around me, and slowly, I drift off to sleep.

But before I fall completely, I hear Nero's voice in a whispered vow.

"I'll keep you safe, I promise. Nobody will ever hurt you again."

Chapter 12

Lily

My bruises heal, and in a couple of days, I barely have a mark to show for my near-death experience. Nero is wary, but I'm determined to carry on as normal.

I'm not just hiding away, waiting for the next disaster to strike.

"If I stay home, they'll think you're running scared," I point out, packing for art class on Monday morning.

"I am scared," Nero says grimly. "I'm fucking terrified they'll come after you again."

"Who says I was the target?" I shoot back. I've been cooped up for days, and I need a taste of real life again. "I've never been to the site before, but you're there all the time. They were probably planning to kill you, and just got me by mistake."

"Gee, comforting," Nero grumbles, but he doesn't stop me leaving, as long as I promise to keep Kyle close and informed of my whereabouts at all times.

"I promise," I reassure him. "I'll be fine."

But as I go about my classes in school, I know that's not

exactly true. I didn't want to add to Nero's worries, but I'm not as confident as I seemed. The elevator incident has shaken me, but more than that, I can see it's shaken Nero too.

And nothing rattles that man.

So is this potential war with the Kovacks what's on his mind? He's been acting distant again. The night of my near-death experience, I hoped that we reached a turning point. Being so thoroughly terrified has a way of putting things into perspective.

But the next day, I could feel him pull away from me. It's disheartening, but when I look into his eyes, I can see the worry there. I just don't think he knows how to deal with it.

And neither do I.

I can't stop thinking about the danger lurking around every corner, the threat that comes with the Barretti life. I knew that deep down that pretending to be normal with Nero couldn't last. As much as the fantasy of George and Mary was fun to joke about, it's just that:

A fantasy.

No matter how much I wish our biggest stresses were bickering over whose turn it is to do the dishes, or how to deal with an annoying neighbor, that's not the kind of life we lead.

The question is, will it ever be? Nero was convinced that striking this deal with the Kovacks and turning legit would remove the threat and herald a new era for the Barretti organization, but this latest attack makes me wonder.

Is this what life will always be like: A new danger lurking around every bend?

I make it through my class, hating that I'm wasting this opportunity to learn about my craft because my mind is a jumble of thoughts that I can't seem to control. I'm walking out to the quad alone when my cell phone rings.

It's Juliet. I brighten. "Hey there," I answer. "Ready for girls' night part two already?"

She laughs. "Absolutely, although I didn't have a hangover to deal with. Mara was grumbling all through work the next day in dark sunglasses."

I smile. "I'm sure she looked amazing. That woman has great style."

"She does. The new collection is in large part down to her," Juliet adds. "Are you guys confirmed for tonight?"

"Tonight?" I echo, confused.

"The Sterling Cross party," Juliet reminds me. "To show off our latest collection in style."

Oh, *right*.

"I'm sorry," I wince. "It completely slipped my mind."

"That's OK, I know the last couple of weeks have been a little overwhelming..."

"A little?" I chuckle. "Don't worry, we'll be there."

"Nero's gracing us with his presence?" Juliet sounds surprised.

"He will once I'm done persuading him," I joke. "In fact, I don't have any classes for the rest of the day, so I'm going to take myself shopping for a new outfit."

"I can't wait to see it. Talk tonight!"

Juliet rings off, and I look around. Kyle is lurking nearby, so I beckon him over. "You're going to hate me for this," I tell him apologetically. "But how do you feel about hitting Fifth Avenue? I have a party dress to buy."

He doesn't look happy, spending the afternoon trailing around designer boutiques is probably the last thing he wants, but he gamely nods. "Whatever you want."

"You're a loyal employee," I laugh, following him to the car. "I'll be sure to ask Nero for a raise!"

. . .

I spend the afternoon shopping, and then the evening at home getting ready. By the time we arrive at the Sterling Cross party, both Nero and I are dressed to the nines: him in his tuxedo, and me in a flowing green gown with a plunging neckline, my hair pinned up in a chic bun on the top of my head.

Of course, he didn't spend hours on hair and makeup, he just pulled a jacket on over his black T-shirt and ran his fingers through his hair. Men.

"Wow, looks amazing," I say brightly as we pull up outside Cipriani 42nd Street. "Juliet said they were going all out, but this is something else."

Nero barely grunts in answer, waiting as I get out of the car. He's been quiet all evening. Distant. I'm hoping a night out on the town will help relax him, and be the distraction he needs, so I take his arm and steer him inside.

The building is large and impressive with its Italian Renaissance design and red carpet leading to the entrance. Inside the event space, there are high ceilings held up with marble columns and breathtaking chandeliers. The inlaid floor is full of people milling around, all dressed in designer clothes and expensive jewelry.

We fit right in.

Cocktails are being served, and we barely make more than five feet into the room before we're stopped by a waiter with a tray of drinks. "Hmmm, I'll take the Cross Cosmopolitan," I decide, ordering from the special menu. "Nero?"

"Nothing for me," he says shortly.

"Are you sure?" I ask.

Nero just waves the waiter away.

"Remember, there are lots of movers and shakers here," I remind him, hoping that if he won't force a smile for me, he'll do it for his business. "Lots of great contacts for you, for the real estate development. Future clients, buyers, who knows...?"

But even that doesn't shift the scowl from his face. I sigh, taking a sip of my drink. So much for a fun night. Still, we're here now, so I guide us through the crowd, stopping and greeting familiar faces from all our social networking of the past months. It's nice not to have an agenda this time, or be angling for certain introductions, and even with Nero silent beside me, I begin to have a good time.

Finally, we reach Juliet and Caleb, who have been holding court by some of the display cases showing off classic Sterling Cross designs. Juliet is beaming as soon as she lays eyes on us.

"I'm so glad you guys could make it," she cries. "Lily, you look beautiful."

"Thank you, and you're a vision, as always."

Juliet looks like a model in her red dress. She's wearing diamond studs in her ears and a teardrop ruby pendant hanging from her necklace.

"Nero," Caleb says with a nod. Nero returns the gesture, and Juliet and I share a smile.

"My god, don't be so expressive," she teases. "You'll make a scene."

Caleb laughs at that, but Nero doesn't even crack a smile.

"There go the plans for a big double date," Juliet continues quipping, clearly at ease with the tension that still lingers between the men: brothers in blood, and reluctant allies. "But I'm going to need more enthusiasm for our big announcement..." She beams wider, as Caleb puts his arm around her, pulling her close. "You already know, Lily, but we're finally sharing the good news with everyone. I'm pregnant!"

I cheer and congratulate them again, giving Juliet a massive hug.

"Congratulations," Nero says quietly. But that's all. I manage to cover for him with excited questions, then suddenly, I see both Juliet and Caleb tense, looking past me.

Ruthless Vow

I turn. A tall, impeccably-dressed man is approaching. Make that, sauntering. Heads turn to watch him, and as he gets closer, I realize I recognize him. It's Sebastian Wolfe, the English hedge-fund billionaire. Nero mentioned him being a business rival, but seeing the reactions from Caleb and Juliet, nobody here is a fan.

"Look, it's all my favorite people," Sebastian says with a smirk, as he draws closer. "Discussing me, are you?"

Juliet glares. "Why would we talk about someone so insignificant? And how did you get in here, anyway? You definitely weren't invited."

Sebastian chuckles in amusement. "I just stopped by to check out your little show. Shame you didn't roll over for me when you had the chance," he says, and Caleb immediately steps up with a growl. Sebastian raises his hands, "Easy there, tiger," he says, clearly enjoying the reaction. "I was talking about Sterling Cross, and my takeover attempt. Obviously. Not that your wife isn't a charming woman," he adds with a wink.

"Get out." Caleb snaps.

"Don't worry, I have more important places to be," Sebastian says, adjusting his tux. He glances to Nero. "The invitation to join my card game is still open. If it's not too rich for your tastes."

I'm expecting a sharp comeback like last-time the two met, but Nero doesn't say a word.

"Suit yourself." Sebastian gives a nod. "Ladies, you have my sympathies, as always."

He strolls away.

Juliet exhales. "I hate that guy," she says, scowling after him.

"What happened with him, anyway?" I ask, curious.

"Oh, hostile takeover, back-stabbing, the usual," she replies. "But Nero fixed it."

"He's good like that," I smile in agreement, but Nero remains stone-faced. When Juliet and Caleb move on to mingle, I sigh.

"Okay, what's going on?" I ask, grabbing Nero's arm to make him turn to face me. "I thought you liked Juliet, but you couldn't even pretend to be happy for her pregnancy news!"

"What do you want from me?" Nero shoots back. "I didn't want to come to this thing, but I'm here. Now I'm supposed to put on a show, turn fucking cartwheels?"

"No," I step back, stung. "I just thought..."

"I'm going to get a drink."

Nero strides off. I watch him go, but he doesn't head for the bar. Instead, he exits through one of the open patio doors, moving outside.

I follow.

I find him standing in the shadows of the terrace away from the crowd, restlessly playing with his cufflinks. "Nero, talk to me," I say, approaching him. "You've been in a terrible mood for days, and I want to know why. Did something happen with the Kovacks?"

"You mean more than the bullshit we're already knee-deep in?"

His harsh tone makes me step back, but I won't be dissuaded. "Talk to me," I say again. "*Please?*"

"Fine." Nero pauses a moment, and reaches into the inner pocket of his tuxedo jacket, pulling out an envelope. "Here."

"What is it?" I take the envelope but don't open it. I want him to *talk* to me.

"A plane ticket to Paris."

"What?" I blink. Of all the things I was expecting him to say, I definitely wasn't expecting this.

"You heard me." Nero watches as I tear the envelope open.

Ruthless Vow

There it is: first class to Paris, leaving tomorrow. "I know you've always wanted to go," he says.

I squeal in excitement, I can't help it. I even bounce up and down on my toes. "Are you serious?" I gasp, already picturing the two of us walking hand-in-hand along the Seine. "Paris?"

"You'll love it," he says quietly. "You can see all the galleries, eat French food, and even study there. I'm sure there are some great art schools in Paris."

I pause, realizing something for the first time. He's saying "you," not "we."

"I don't understand." I ask, confused. "Aren't you coming?"

Nero shakes his head. "No. No, I'm not."

"But..." I come back down to earth with a bump, trying to make sense of it. "Is this just to get me away while things die down here?" I ask, hopefully. "A month away, until the danger has passed?"

Nero swallows, finally meeting my eyes. "No. It's not just for a month, Lily, you're going for good. I've set everything up for you, I got you an apartment, completely in your name. Visas, everything. And I'll be moving money to a bank account for you, too. You'll have a whole life there, the one you've always wanted. Far away from all this bullshit."

Far away from him.

I stand there, gripping the ticket. I can't believe what he's saying, I don't understand. "But what about you?" I ask.

But I already know. It's in the hardness of his face and the cold stare he levels at me.

"I'm staying here. I'll file for divorce. It's over."

Chapter 13
Lily

The world stops spinning.

I'm more than stunned. I'm frozen, my heart in my throat.

It's over.

That's what he said. Before I can even begin to process his exclamation, Nero turns away and heads back into the party. I'm left standing there with the envelope in my hand, the one that contains the future that Nero has chosen for me.

A solo future. Without him.

My heart aches. He's really packing me off and shipping me away. And as much as I've wanted to walk away a hundred times since arriving back in his life, this is the wakeup call I can't deny.

I love him. I belong with him.

Forever.

I may not have meant my vows when I took them, under duress, but I feel them now, in my heart. He's the only man I've ever loved. And I won't let him push me away.

Snapping out of my daze, I head back into the party. I frantically scan the crowd, looking for any sign of him, but I don't see him anywhere.

He's left.

I charge outside, my anger rising. Kyle is waiting on the curb, like he was expecting me.

"Where is he?" I demand, reaching up and pulling the clip out of my hair that keeps it pulled back tightly. The blonde locks come tumbling down around my shoulders.

"Nero?" Kyle looks wary.

"No, I'm trying to find Brad Pitt, you seen him?"

Kyle sighs. "He didn't say where he was going. Came out about ten minutes ago and caught a cab."

"A cab? Why would he do that?"

"Why would I know? He's your husband."

Kyle is just kidding around, but his words cause pain to punch a hole in my chest.

I swallow back a sob. "Just take me home, please," I ask quietly, scrambling into the car. I'll apologize to Juliet later for bailing without saying goodbye, but I know that I can't stay another minute and pretend like my heart isn't breaking.

Why would he do this?

I keep replaying Nero's words in my head. *It's over.* Just like that. Like I'm one of his loyal employees, to boss around as he sees fit.

My shock and heartache shift to anger, as I realize he must have been planning this for days. Planning *my* life.

How dare he?

My rage builds with every city block, and the minute we pull up outside the townhouse, I climb out of the car and storm inside. I find Nero in the living room, sitting in the chair in front of the fireplace with a newly opened bottle of scotch in his hand. He slumps, drinking straight from the bottle as I stalk over and plant myself in front of him, my hands on my hips.

"That's it?" I demand, icy. "You think you're just going to declare us over and be done with it?"

Nero's gaze hardens. "It's what you've wanted, all along," he says, taking another swig from the bottle. "We made a bargain when I brought you here: Your help getting the land deal, in exchange for my protection. As far as I'm concerned, you've fulfilled your obligation. You're off the hook. I won't come after you or Teddy. It's done."

I inhale sharply. Everything we've been through; he's just reduced it to a few short sentences. Bargains. Obligation. An exchange.

"What about *us*?" I demand, my voice twisting with emotion. "I'm your wife now!"

"And that was a mistake." Nero gets to his feet, pacing. "Just let this go, Princess. I told you, it's over."

"Stop saying that!" I hate the way my voice cracks. I feel like I'm completely exposed, my emotions laid out for him to see. And he's just watching me with cool indifference. As if he never held me as I fell asleep, or swore he loved me, after all.

I take a deep breath and try to reason with him. "Listen, I know why you're doing this. I get it. You're scared for my safety, but this isn't the answer. You don't have to send me away," I continue, pleading. "We can get through this. Together."

But Nero's eyes are cold. "Grow up, Princess. I told you, the fantasy of a normal life was just for one day. I'm a Baretti. You'll never be safe with me."

His mask slips. I see the fear before he hardens again. I know that I'm right. He's doing this because he thinks it'll protect me.

"What if I don't want a normal life?" I demand, moving closer, so that only mere inches separate us. "What if I just want you?"

I place my palms on his chest, feeling the heat of his body through the thin tuxedo shirt.

He shakes his head, looking tormented. "It's not that easy."

"But we're supposed to be together. You told me. You promised!"

I reach up, desperately pulling him down so I can kiss him. Trying to show him the passion that binds us. The connection I could never deny. For a moment, he's frozen there, unyielding, but then his resistance wavers as I press closer, arching my body against him.

His stern lips soften as I ply them with kisses. His hands move to my waist, and I use the opportunity to wrap my arms around his neck, wanting to strip away his defenses. Needing to—

"No!" Nero tears himself away from me. "That's enough," he swears. "It's over, Lily. Hell, it was never even real."

He walks out, slamming the front door behind him.

No.

My legs give way and I sink to the couch. I can't believe it, but he's made his mind up. He's determined to send me away.

But how does this make any sense? I'm still a target, wherever I am in the world. Here, at least, I have Nero's security. Kyle, and his men, and Nero himself ready to take on anyone who tries to hurt me.

But in Paris, I'll be alone. The distance won't stop anyone, I'll be a sitting duck for the first person who wants to send a message to the great Nero Barretti. A divorce agreement won't change that. I'll still be in danger.

Without him.

My heart aches. For all the talk of safety and protection, that's not the real reason my heart is breaking in my chest right now. No, it's because Nero has chosen a life without me. After swearing all this time that I belonged to him, that he was the only man who could make me happy, he's ready to just give up on us. Like I'm better off without him loving me.

But he can't truly believe that…

Can he?

I don't want to wait until it's too late to find out. I quickly change out of my gown into jeans and a sweater, grab Nero's keys and slip out the back door, exiting through the alley and climbing in the car he keeps parked there. I drive over to the club, suspecting he'll be there. It's home turf to him, the place where he's boss, and everybody knows better than to talk back.

But I still have a few things to say.

The bar is full of people, so busy that I'm able to slip through the crowded room without anyone really noticing me. My thoughts are full of possible arguments, ways to convince him to see reason, as I hurry down the back hallway to his office. His door is ajar, and I push it open without thinking, about to launch into my fervent pleas—

"Ooh, baby, look at you."

A woman's voice snaps me back to reality. I gasp in shock. Nero is here, just as I suspected. But he's not alone.

He's leaning against his desk, knuckles white as he grips the wood. And there's a woman on her knees in front of him, some blonde I don't recognize, breasts spilling out of a tight red dress, cooing in a breathy voice as she unzips his pants.

I freeze. "Nero?" I say, my voice coming out a whisper.

His eyes meet mine, and I almost don't recognize him, the expression in his gaze is so distant and cold. "Yeah?" he asks, casual. Like there isn't a woman down on the floor about to blow him.

Like my heart isn't being ripped out of my chest.

"What... What are you doing?"

Tears sting in my eyes, but I can't move. Can't breathe. Can't do anything but stand there in the doorway, watching him take our love and burn it all to the ground.

The woman twists, eyes widening as she sees me there. "Oh shit." She starts to pull away, but Nero stops her, placing a hand on the back of her head.

"Don't," he says. "Keep going."

I watch, aghast, as she does as she's told, kissing her way down his stomach. He gives me a cruel smirk, over her head. "What did you think, Lily? That your pampered Princess routine can give a man what he really needs? You don't even come close to satisfying me. And playing pretend gets old fast."

I reel back, dizzy. I think I'm going to be sick. "You love me," I say weakly, even though the evidence right in front of me tells a different story.

"Maybe once," he shrugs. "Back when I was young and too cunt-struck to know what love is, but that was a long time ago. I know better now."

"Nero, please..." I find myself begging.

"Please, what?" he gives a cruel laugh. "Aww, are you going to cry and pout, and beg me to stay? You're too late, Princess. I'm already counting down the minutes until you get on that damn plane. Then finally I'll be free to have some real fun. Isn't that right, baby?" he asks the woman below him, deliberately wrapping her hair in his hands. "Be sure to take every inch," he tells her. "Suck it good. Put on a real nice show for my wife here, yeah?"

The woman giggles, pushing his pants down. "Whatever floats your boat," she coos.

Oh my God, she's going to start blowing him right in front of me. I stagger back, tears swimming in my eyes.

"You're awful," I sob. My heart can't take anymore.

I tried. I fought for him, for *us*. But it turns out that he's right.

It's over.

I turn and flee.

Chapter 14

Nero

The minute Lily finally rushes out of the office, I shove the woman away before she can even touch my cock.

"Stop, please." I bark, my heart pounding. Bile rises in the back of my throat, and I have to grip the desk to keep from retching.

Fuck.

I can't believe I just did that. But even though it was the plan to send Lily running, it doesn't make it any easier.

"So, you don't want a blowjob?" the woman asks, confused. She gets to her feet.

"No." I pull out my wallet and grab a couple of hundreds. "I can't. Take your money and go."

She shrugs, plucking the money from my hand. "Whatever. Easiest money I ever made. Call me if you want me *not* to blow you again," she adds, with a wink, strutting out the door.

I can't even look at her. All I see right now is the look on Lily's face when she opened the door. The betrayal. The pain.

The utter heartache.

I know how she feels, even if she'll be cursing my name now for all eternity.

Fuck.

I find the nearest bottle and take a long gulp. Whiskey. The alcohol burns going down, but it's nowhere near enough to overpower my guilt and shame.

This is what you wanted. A voice reminds me. *This is why you set the whole thing up.*

I take another gulp, filled with self-loathing. Yeah, I planned this. Just to hurt her. I knew she'd come looking for me. I knew she'd try and talk me into letting her stay. And fuck it, I knew, that if she gazed up at me with those big blue eyes, and put her hands on my body, and whispered she was mine, I'd fold.

She's my biggest weakness. my greatest liability.

And the only one who matters in the whole goddamn world.

I'd do anything to keep her safe from harm—even breaking both our hearts to make it happen.

And now, I have.

She hates me. I could see it written all over her beautiful face. She'll never forgive me for what she thinks I've done with that woman—and that's the point. Nothing happened, but I need to make sure that once she goes, she stays gone, hating me until the day I die. Because she may not see it now, but she's better off without me. She'll get to live the life she deserves, far away from my twisted world. I can't keep putting her in danger, just by loving her.

I have to protect her. And that means saying goodbye.

So why does it feel so wrong, pushing her away?

I shake my head. It doesn't matter what I feel. This is the plan, and I'm sticking to it. I'll make sure our divorce is public knowledge, and she'll be out of the city. If everyone knows we're not together anymore, she should be safe.

That's worth any pain I might have cause her or myself. As much as I feel like a piece of myself just died, I'd rather break my own heart a thousand times than see her hurt again—or worse, dead.

I look around. I don't want to stay in this room a moment longer, but I can't face the thought of going home.

Home.

It's not going to feel like a home anymore. Lily's flight is tomorrow, and after what just happened, I'm sure she won't miss it.

Then, what'll be left for me at that house? *Fuck.* I realize that I'm not ever going to be able to face that building again. I bought it for her. To give her the kind of palace she deserved. Now, it'll just be a large, empty space with reminders of her around every corner. The moments I got to hold her.

The few, precious nights we shared together in my bed.

I drink again—and I don't stop. The only thing that'll help me now is oblivion, and it can't come soon enough. I've loved that woman since I was seventeen, and I'll keep on loving her until the day I die, but she's out of reach now. I'll never see her again.

Lily's gone.

Chapter 15

Lily

I don't see Nero again. He didn't come home all night, but maybe I shouldn't be surprised. He was probably too busy fucking that woman somewhere.

And I was too busy weeping on the bathroom floor.

I couldn't sleep, I kept replaying every ugly detail, from the sight of her hands on his body, to the cruel, heartless glint in his eye. Taunting me.

Making a mockery of the love we shared.

How could he do it?

Betraying me with another woman. The one thing he knew would shatter my trust forever.

By the time morning light filters through the open drapes, I've driven myself crazy wondering why. But the 'why' doesn't matter. He's made his choice.

And now I have to make mine.

I drag myself off the floor, splash cold water on my face, and pack, not paying much attention to what I throw into the open suitcase. Everything I own has come from Nero, and I don't want to be personally attached to any of it. I don't want to be attached to *him*.

A day ago, heading to Paris would have been a dream come true, but now, it feels like a consolation prize. But still, I try to talk myself into it. The art, the culture, the foreign streets I've been painting all these years… Who knows, maybe having an entire ocean between us will help break this hold he has on me?

I can only dream.

My cab arrives, so I haul my bag downstairs, but I still pause in the doorway. Wondering if Nero will come and try to make me stay.

But the house is empty. I'm all alone.

Just the way I've been for years.

Get it together, Lily, I tell myself. *You have a chance for a fresh start now.*

I leave my keys on the table and go.

The ride to the airport passes in a blur. I can't help thinking of the very different trip I took to arrive in New York: Tied up in the back of a van, Nero's captive. I had no idea what lay ahead of me—or that the man I'd been running from for half my life would become the only man I wanted to run *towards*.

Coming face-to-face with Nero again changed everything, and soon enough, I couldn't hide from our connection. My hatred and my anger were just a defense mechanism, trying to protect my heart from the love I'd always felt for him. Ever since I was younger and didn't even fully know what love meant.

But now I do.

My broken heart aches in my chest, and despite the depths of my grief, I long for him to be sitting beside me. For us to be embarking on this new adventure together—instead of me facing my future alone.

Without him.

When I get to the airport, it's busy and packed with travelers. I make my way to the first class check-in. "Travelling alone?" the perky attendant asks me.

I wince. "Yes."

"Departure is on time," she says, checking my bag. "The first class lounge is on the second floor, near gate 20."

I nod my thanks, and take my ticket, heading over to the long, winding line for security. With my VIP ticket, I'm ushered to the fast-track lane, where only a couple of people are waiting in front of me.

It's a young couple, practically glowing with love and happiness.

"I can't wait to open the wedding gifts. Did you see how full the table was?" the woman asks.

"Not at all. I was too distracted by how beautiful you looked in your dress." I see the guy slide his hand over her ass.

Newlyweds.

My heart sinks, aching with longing.

The woman giggles, and it's a pure, happy sound. "Mom's dropping the gifts off at the apartment, so they'll be waiting when we get back from the Maldives."

"I can't wait to see you in that new bikini."

They whisper and giggle, love radiating. I can't look away, not until they're whisked through the security barriers and off to the rest of their lives together.

That should be me and Nero. It should be us.

"Next."

I realize the guard is beckoning to me. "Sorry," I blurt, hurrying forwards. He nods me through the metal detectors, and they sound a bleep of alarm.

"Keys, jewelry?" the female agent moves forward.

I shake my head, still distracted.

She sighs impatiently. "Your wedding ring?" she reminds me.

I glance down. "Oh. Sorry. I forgot."

I realize that I'm still wearing the wedding ring Nero gave me. I slide it off, and stand there a moment, staring at the ring. I could just leave it here. After all, it doesn't mean anything anymore—at least, not to Nero.

He made it clear to me, our arrangement is over. And now, our marriage is, too.

But holding the simple gold band, I feel a new resolve form in my veins.

A certainty, as clear as oxygen.

It's not over.

"Ma'am?" the guard prompts me.

"Just a minute," I blurt, my mind racing.

Nero's pushing me away, doing whatever it takes to get me out of the country and away from him. But I don't have to accept it.

Why does *he* get to make my choice?

Despite what he did last night, I still believe he wants to protect me. In fact, it's *because* he's so worried for my safety that he probably set up that whole stunt with the other woman. I was too shocked and heartbroken to see it in the moment, but looking back now, it makes perfect sense.

He wants me to be angry with him, so he did the one thing guaranteed to make me leave. Pushing me away, all the way to another continent is supposed to be a way to keep me safe.

He doesn't realize that there's no safer place for me than in his arms.

"Ma'am," the guard says, sounding annoyed now. "You're holding up the line."

I feel a surge of adrenaline, pumping in my veins. I back away from the screening gate. "I... I need to go back."

"What?"

"I'm not going," I blurt, "I'm not leaving him."

The guard rolls his eyes, like he gets this nonsense all the time. "Fine," he scowls, "Which one is your bag?"

I point it out, and he hauls it back and hands it over. "Next!" he yells, already forgetting me, as I turn and fight my way around the line behind me.

I'm not going.

I'm not leaving him.

I practically sprint back through the airport the way I came, my certainty growing with every step. This is the right choice.

This is *my* choice.

Because when do I get to call the shots in my own life? I never really have. My dad was in charge when I was young, making his deal with the FBI that sent us to the other side of the country without any input from me whatsoever. Ever since, the Barrettis have been the biggest influence over my life. They are the reason that I was always on edge and ready to run. The reason that I lived in fear for so many years.

But I'm sick of running. Hiding. Letting other people push me around. I won't do it anymore. It's my life, to spend however I want.

I choose a life with him.

I hightail out of the terminal and jump in a cab, giving the address for Nero's club. My heart is pounding now, with excitement and nerves.

If he thinks this is over, he's got another thing coming. I'm not going to make it so easy on him. He wants to be the asshole to drive me away? Then, he's going to have to up his game. Because I'm coming to fight for what I want.

And this time, I'm going to win.

. . .

Ruthless Vow

The ride flies by, and soon, we're pulling up at the bar. I tumble out of the cab and burst inside, not slowing as I race to his office. I'm fired up, and ready for the confrontation, for Nero to flip his shit, but when I throw his office door open, the room is empty.

Dammit.

I pause, thinking fast.

"Lily?"

I turn, it's Avery, looking surprised to see me. "I thought you'd be sipping champagne in first class by now," she says, offering me a sympathetic smile.

I shake my head. "Have you seen Nero?"

"He just left," she says. "He was heading to the site, then home."

I smile. "Thank you!" I call back to her, already flying down the hallway and out the back door.

I hurry down the steps into the grimy alleyway, then stop, happy to see Kyle loitering on his usual cigarette break. "Hey," I greet him.

He does a double take. "Oh shit," he says, with a grin. "Trouble's back in town. I told the boss it wouldn't be so easy to get rid of you."

"It seems like you're the only one not underestimating me." I smile.

"Yeah, that seems like a recipe for disaster." He drops his cigarette, and stubs it out with his heel. "You need a ride? I'd like to see the look on his face—"

BANG.

Out of nowhere, a bullet hits him, square in the forehead. Kyle's blood paints the wall behind him. He slumps to the ground, eyes still open, but not seeing anything.

Dead.

My jaw drops. *What the fuck just happened?*

I stand frozen in shock, not believing my eyes. Then my instincts override everything.

I scream, lurching away from the body. *The bullet came from behind me.* I start to turn to see who's there, who did this, but before I can, something heavy hits the back of my head.

A blinding pain shoots through me. My knees buckle and darkness floods my mind.

I'm unconscious before I hit the ground.

Chapter 16
Lily

Darkness.

I wake, confused and in pain. I'm crammed in a confined space. My head is throbbing, and I can't move, and I struggle to put together what's going on.

I was at the club, and then—

Kyle.

Oh my God. The fear crashes through me, recalling the blood-splatter, and the blank look in his eyes as he fell to the ground.

Whoever shot him, they hit me over the head, and brought me...

Where, exactly?

I force myself to breathe, squinting around in the dim light. I'm lying on my side in a dark space, not big enough to stretch out. My hands are tied behind my back, and I can feel motion, and hear the sounds of traffic.

A car, I realize. I'm locked in the trunk of a car. I wriggle, trying to move, just as the car travels over uneven terrain, making my head bump into the floor of the trunk. Sharp pain slices through the back of my skull, and I have to bite my lip to keep from crying out.

Who took me? And where are they taking me?

I try to think clearly. Is it the Kovacks? Did they really betray Nero and come after me? Or is it some other threat?

Will they kill me, the way they killed Kyle?

I feel my anxiety rise, until I can barely breathe. I panic, struggling wildly, but that just throws me around the trunk, bashing painfully at the interior.

Focus, I order myself. I can't just give up, no matter how grim things are.

I need to get free.

Forcing myself to take a deep breath, and then another, I flex my wrists behind me, testing the bonds. It's some kind of electrical tape, too solid to break. Dammit. Trapped behind my back, my hands are of no use to me.

Unless...

I twist onto my side in the small space, bringing my knees up tight against my chest. By curling tightly into a ball, I'm able to bring my bound hands underneath my ass and legs, so they're tied in front of me, instead of behind.

Now, at least, I can use them.

Carefully, I feel all around the interior of the trunk. It's empty, save a blanket, and some papers. But don't trunks have a wheel well?

I scoot to one side, running my fingertips around the edge of the fabric floor until I can peel it up. I reach around blindly underneath, until my hands land on something metallic and hard. I run my fingers over it eagerly, gripping it in both hands.

A lug wrench.

I lie back, clutching it to my chest. I have a weapon. Now, all I can do is wait as the car keeps moving. Eventually, we make a turn, and the smoother ride of the highway turns uneven and rough. We bounce along, slowing, until finally, it comes to a stop.

I feel fear slip down my spine. *This is it.* My heart is racing as the engine is cut off. I hear the car door open and close, and I adjust my sweaty palm on the lug wrench, heart pounding.

I'll have one chance, that's it. The benefit of surprise.

Footsteps crunch around the side of the car. There's the small sound of metal on metal as the trunk is unlocked. Then the trunk pops open.

I don't hesitate. I rear up, swinging wildly with everything I have. There's a dull THWACK of impact as I hit someone, and they go reeling back.

"You fucking bitch!" The man howls. I scramble out of the trunk, as he straightens, fury on his familiar face.

It's Chase.

What the fuck?!

I don't stick around to ask questions, I take off running, my sneakers pounding on the grass. We're in a woodland clearing, nothing but trees around and a dirt track running through the woods. *Fuck.*

"Get back here!" Chase follows. I hear him behind me, his long legs eating up the space between us quickly. I barely make it twenty feet before he grabs my arm and yanks me around. I scream, swinging wildly, but I'm no match for his bulk and fighting skills. He grabs the wrench from me and tosses it aside. "Nice try," he growls, sneering.

With no weapon, I use the only thing I have: my hands. I scratch at him wildly, tearing at the skin of his neck. He bellows in pain. "Bitch!"

Then he balls up his fist and punches me in the face.

Owwww.

Pain explodes in my cheekbone, and I would drop to the ground from the force of impact if he weren't holding me up.

"No more fucking surprises," he says, roughly dragging me back the way we came. "I need you alive for now, but you could spare a few limbs."

I stagger behind him, barely keeping stride. My ears are ringing, and my head aches, trying to process everything.

I don't understand.

Chase has never liked me, but he's loyal to Nero. His oldest friend. A Barretti man.

So why does he want to hurt me? Why would he murder Kyle in cold blood?

Just what is he planning?

Chase drags me past the car, to where an old log cabin is half-hidden in the trees. It has a sagging roof and a boarded-up window in the front. The grass and weeds are overgrown, and when his heavy footsteps land on the porch steps, the wood creaks like it might collapse at any moment.

Inside, it's just as decrepit. It's a little, one-bedroom cabin with shabby furniture and a thick layer of dust on everything. I look around, chilled by the scene. We're in the middle of nowhere here, like something out of a horror movie. I need to think fast.

Chase grabs a wooden chair at the tiny kitchen table and drags it to the center of the room. He throws me down on it, and pulls out a wicked looking switchblade.

I gasp. "It's OK, I get the message! I'm not going anywhere."

"Too fucking right," Chase scowls. He advances, reaching for me—

And slices the tape from my wrists.

Before I can relax, or rub the injured skin, he grabs a length of rope, and ties me to the chair, binding my wrists to each arm and tying my ankles to the wood, too. The ropes cut harshly into my skin, but I try not to show pain as he yanks my bindings even tighter.

"I don't know what's going on here," I say, my voice trembling. "But take a moment. Talk to me. I'm sure we can work it out."

His laugh is cold.

"Work this out? You really are a piece of work. Is the Princess going to offer to blow me to get out of her predicament?"

I want to gag. "That's not what I meant. Just... Just untie me, and we can have a conversation."

Chase scowls. He touches his neck, wincing at the broken skin my nails managed to catch. "The only reason you're not dead yet is I might need proof the Kovacks have taken you."

"*What?*" I blurt. "You're working for them?"

Chase snorts. "Not in a million years. Because unlike your traitor husband, I don't break bread with the fucking enemy."

He's angry—but not just at me. I watch him, trying to figure this out. Because until I know what's going on, I can't find a way out of it.

"So tell me, what are you trying to do?" I urge him, keeping my voice soft. "Maybe I can help?"

"Help?" Chase whirls around, furious. His face is contorted in rage. "You're the one who's ruined everything! Nero's turning his back on his family for you, giving up everything this organization fought for. Everything we bled for!"

I shiver in fear. He's breathing heavily, wild-eyed. He's lost control, pacing and ranting like a madman.

"But I can get him back," Chase continues. "I can fix this. See, once he thinks the Kovacks killed you, he'll do what needs to be done. He'll remember what matters and defend the Baretti name. The stupid détente will be called off, and we can wipe out our rivals for good. The old way," he vows.

"It was you, wasn't it?" I realize. "You sabotaged the elevator at the construction site. And you tried to get Nero to believe it was the Kovacks."

I'm putting the pieces together now, and I feel sick. Nero trusts Chase like a brother. He has no idea what the guy's been plotting behind his back.

Chase turns toward the door, and the thought of being alone in this isolated place makes me feel like a fist is squeezing my stomach. "Where are you going?" I blurt, afraid.

"I need to get back to Nero. He'll need his lieutenant for the upcoming war." Chase says it with satisfaction. "Don't worry, Princess. I'll be back for you."

He slams the door behind him, and a moment later, I hear the sound of the car engine. He drives away.

Silence.

I swallow hard. There's no way I can be here waiting when he gets back. The man has lost grip on reality, and there's no saying what he'll do. He's already killed one person to put this plan into action.

Who knows when he'll decide to get rid of me, too?

I start trying to loosen my binds, but it's useless. The ropes are too tight. So, I wait another few minutes, just to be safe, and then I start yelling for help.

"Hello?" I cry. "Is anyone out there? HELP!"

I know it's a long shot. I didn't see any signs of life nearby, and Chase wouldn't have picked this cabin to hide me unless he was sure I wouldn't be found.

But still, I scream. I yell, and shriek until my voice is hoarse, echoing into the trees.

No response. Nobody's coming.

I sink back, exhausted now. Darkness is falling outside the cabin, and I can't tell how much time has passed, but I must have been here for hours. I look around, for something I can use to get through the ropes, but the place is bare. There's nothing but me, and the rickety chair, and the hard wooden floor.

This is going to hurt.

I hold my breath as I hurl myself to the side, knocking the chair to the ground with a bang that makes my bones vibrate. The chair shakes, but it stays intact. So, I haul myself up, and do it again.

And again.

Every time sends pain shooting through my body, but I don't stop. I'll break my own bones all night if it means smashing this chair and getting free.

I have to get out of here and warn Nero. I know, the minute he thinks that the Kovacks have taken me, he'll unleash hell on earth to get me back.

I have to get free before it's too late.

Chapter 17

Nero

"So, we're on target?" I demand. I'm in a meeting with Miles and my accountants, going over the projections for the construction site. "I don't like these overtime numbers..."

"You can either have it cheap, or you can have it fast," one of the numbers guys offers. "You'll pay a premium now, but it'll be worth it to get the place finished sooner."

Another guy nods. "We budgeted for this. If you take a look at page seventeen..."

I zone out as they start discussing tax breaks and depreciation. I should be loving this, I'm usually all about the details, but today my mind's a million miles away.

Across the Atlantic. With Lily.

She should have landed by now, I reckon. I wonder if she's still furious at me, or if the excitement of the foreign city has taken the edge off her heartbreak.

I hope so. I don't want her burdened with this pain for long. I can carry it for the both of us.

I'll bear it until the day I die.

"Let's wrap things up," I announce, bringing the meeting to a close. "Gentlemen…"

They collect their files, and head out. "Wait up, Miles," I stop him before he exits with the rest of them. "You clean everything up with the bookkeeper?"

"What?" he startles, eyes wide.

"You know, that missing money," I remind him. "Tell them I need everything squared away, now the development's full-steam ahead. Can't risk an audit, or anything with the IRS."

"Right." Miles clears his throat, looking pale. "Yeah, sorry, I forgot to call. Will chase it down, no problem."

"Good." I nod. "And have them double-check last quarter, too. A hundred k here, another hundred there… Shit like that shouldn't be falling through the cracks. If someone around here has sticky fingers, I need to know."

His head bobs in a nod. "Yes, boss."

Miles takes off, and I look at my desk full of paperwork and sigh. Every file and folder on there represents tens of millions of dollars in projects, cash that's going to be pouring into the Barretti coffers. Hell, I've toiled for years to make this new development happen. I should be on top of the world right now.

But instead of enjoying my success, it's a hollow victory.

Everything's hollow without her.

I leave the work and make my way down the hallway to the main bar. It's busy, and I need to catch a buzz if I'm going to face another night alone, thinking of Lily.

I take a seat on a stool, and the man behind the bar automatically grabs the bottle of Macallan that's kept behind the bar just for me. It's expensive shit, but it goes down smooth.

"Another?" the bartender asks, eying me as I knock the glass back in one.

I nod.

"I didn't expect to see you here today."

I turn as Avery joins me at the bar. "Is Lily meeting you?"

I frown at her. "Of course not," I say curtly. "You know she's in Paris by now."

Avery looks surprised. "But I thought she decided not to go."

My hand freezes, glass halfway to my lips. "What are you talking about?"

"She was here yesterday, looking for you," Avery explains. "I figured you've been locked up together, celebrating your reunion all night."

I shake my head, confused. "I haven't seen her. She didn't..."

I pull out my phone and check, but there are no calls, no messages. I try her number, but it goes straight to voicemail.

I turn back to Avery. "When was this?" I demand.

Her eyes widen. "Umm, I don't know, about noon?"

"And where did she go after that?" I get to my feet.

"I don't know." Avery shrugs. "I'm sorry, I just passed her in the hallway. That's it."

Fuck.

"What's wrong?" Avery asks, reading my mind.

I shake my head. "I don't know, but something's not right. It doesn't make sense. If Lily didn't get on that flight, then where is she?"

And why isn't she answering her phone?

"Call Lily," I order Avery. "Maybe she's just ignoring *me*."

She doesn't hesitate or waste time asking questions. Turning on the speakerphone, she holds the phone out so I can hear it ring. When the voicemail picks up, I let out a frustrated growl, running my hand through my hair.

"What's going on, boss?" Chase asks, sauntering over to us.

"I don't know where Lily is." I reply shortly. "She didn't get on her flight, nobody's seen her since yesterday."

"Oh shit," his eyes widen. "You think something's happened? Someone's taken her?"

"I don't know what to think," I reply, but the idea he suggests makes my blood run cold.

Taken...

"Why don't you track her phone?" Chase suggests.

I exhale. "Great idea." I pull up the tracking app I had installed on her cellphone, back when she was ready to bolt any chance she got. I'd forgotten I even had it, we're so far past that, but now I'm glad I took the precaution.

"What does it say?" Chase says, crowding in to look. It takes a moment to load the location of Lily's iPhone, but when I see the pin on the map on-screen, my whole world stops.

"Fuck."

"Where is it?" Avery asks.

"Brooklyn. East side." I answer shortly.

"Kovack headquarters." Chase translates. "Motherfuckers. They've got her."

I hear a roaring sound. My heart pounding in my ears.

I did this. I trusted people I shouldn't have. I sent her away and put her in danger. And now...

Now...

Fuck.

If I'd kept her by my side, she wouldn't have been alone. The Kovacks wouldn't have had the opportunity to take her. To do... Whatever they're doing.

Is she hurt? Scared?

Is she even still breathing?

"Goddamnit," I roar, slamming my fist into the nearest wall. It hurts like hell, but I welcome the pain.

I deserve it.

"We can take them," Chase vows. "Those fuckers won't know what hit them."

I nod, leaving my anger and fear right here in the bar. There's no room for emotion now. I need to be a fucking warrior. Merciless.

"Gear up," I order, striding out of the room. I head into the back of the building, down to the basement storage room that's intended for bar supplies.

I use it for a different kind of storage.

I throw open the hidden closet, revealing rows of firearms and ammo. Chase follows me in, kneeling down to a low trunk for a laser-scope rifle, his weapon of choice. As he bends over, I catch a glimpse of some raw-looking scratches, all along his neck.

Chase straightens and sees me looking. "Oh, yeah," he says quickly, his hand reaching up to gingerly touch the wound. "Had a wild night with a real hellcat. Those fucking talons, they do some damage, am I right?" he gives a laugh.

"Sure." I nod, but something in his expression makes me pause. He finishes arming up and turns to me with a grim smile.

"I'll go round up the guys, let them know we're going to war tonight," he says.

"We can't go charging in, guns blazing," I remind him. "Not if there's a chance Lily's still alive."

"That's a long shot, wouldn't you say?" Chase replies. I flinch. "Sorry, man," he adds, slapping my shoulder. "I know it's hard to hear, but we'll make those bastards pay for killing her. Show them what it means to fuck with us."

He heads out, and I watch him go. Something doesn't feel right. An instinct, honed by a lifetime fighting Barretti wars. I can't explain it, but something makes me grab my gun and head up the stairs, a careful distance behind him.

I exit the building out the back door, just in time to see Chase's Charger speed away. I quickly climb into my car, and follow, leaving a couple of cars between us as he moves through the busy downtown streets.

It doesn't take long to confirm that Chase isn't going to collect any of our guys. He takes the Lincoln Tunnel instead, and then hits the freeway, heading north. Upstate.

Where the hell is he going?

He keeps on driving, and I keep pace behind. Every mile takes me further from the city, from that GPS location that showed Lily's phone, but I can't bring myself to turn back. Maybe I'm on a wild goose chase here, but I can't shake the feeling that something's amiss about her being held at the Kovack HQ.

Because it doesn't make sense.

Igor Kovack gave me his word we had a truce. And sure, that may not mean shit to most people, but it was in their interests, too. They have a hell of a lot to gain from seeing our deal through—and even more to lose.

They know me. The Barretti reputation speaks for itself. They know I can burn their fucking world to the ground. So why suddenly fuck things up by taking Lily—the one thing guaranteed to turn me into a vicious killing machine?

But if they didn't take her... Who did?

There's a grim suspicion building in my veins, but I'm trying not to get ahead of myself here. After about an hour of driving, Chase turns off the main highway, and takes a series of country roads, away from the nearest town. We're in the woods now, and I have to drop even further back to keep from being seen.

Finally, he turns down a dirt path. I ease to the side of the road and park, then jog quietly on foot, watching his progress ahead of me through the trees.

He pulls up outside a dilapidated cabin and gets out. He strolls up the front door, and unlocks it, but barely a moment later, he emerges again, looking panicked. He pauses on the porch and looks wildly around, then he tears off into the woods.

What the fuck?

I wait until he's out of sight before slipping through the undergrowth towards the cabin. Chase left the door wide open, so it's easy for me to climb the porch steps and just walk right in.

"Lily?" I call, looking around. But the place is empty.

I flip on the lights, searching for a sign that she might have been here.

And I find it.

The broken remains of a wooden chair lay shattered on the floor, smashed to shit, bearing the remains of rope ties. Someone was kept hostage here. *Lily.*

There's something smudged on the floorboards, and I kneel down to take a closer look.

Chase's name is written there, smeared in some dark liquid.

Blood.

My heart stops. That motherfucker.

I'm on my feet again in an instant, charging out of the cabin. My gun's in my hand, and my whole being is consumed with a single purpose.

Find her. Protect her.

"Lily!" I roar, echoing into the trees. "Lily, I'm coming!"

And my God, Chase is going to pay.

Chapter 18
Lily

I *have to get away.*
 I stumble through the sunny woods, terror making my heart race so loud, it drowns out the sound of my feet crunching over dried brush and sticks. I know I should keep quiet, but I don't have time.
 Chase is coming.
 It took me all night to get free, finally breaking the chair enough to get loose of the bindings, and use a dull rusty knife from the kitchen to saw through the last of the rope. By the time I could limp to the door, I could hear a car engine approaching in the distance.
 So I ran.
 Now, I'm hurtling through the woods, praying with everything I have that I can find civilization—before Chase finds me. Every step sends pain slamming through my body, but I stumble on, heading blindly through the trees.
 Suddenly, my ankle twists on a rock, and I tumble to the ground, stifling a yelp of pain. My hands slam in the dirt, and I lay there, gasping for air in the undergrowth.

It all feels too much. I'm exhausted, and bruised, and I'm stranded in the middle of the woods with a madman determined to kill me. After everything I've been through, I just want to stay right here, but I know that I can't.

Get up, I try and tell myself, but my body doesn't obey. *Get up. You made it this far. You can't give up now.*

"Lily!"

I tense. Someone's yelling my name out there—getting closer. *Fuck.*

I force myself to my feet again and keep running—away from the sound. This is my one chance to get away, and I'm so scared that I'm not going to make it. Desperation is thick in my blood, driving me to move faster, no matter what.

"Lily!"

The voice comes again, louder and clearer this time, and makes me stop in my tracks.

It couldn't be... Could it?

Nero.

Relief crashes through me. He came. He figured out what Chase was planning.

He's here to help me.

I reverse course, heading back the way I came, towards where the shouting came from. If I can just get to him, I can—

OOF!

Someone tackles me out of nowhere, knocking me to the ground. It's Chase! "You think you can get away?" he roars, struggling to pin me in the dirt. "Stay the fuck down!"

I scream.

"Nero!" I yell, clawing wildly at Chase's face. He's too heavy, I can't breathe, but I flail and kick with everything I have. I feel my knee connect with his groin and he cries out in pain.

"Bitch!" he yells, shifting his weight.

The move is enough for me to squirm out from underneath him. I manage to get my upper body free, but my legs are suddenly pinned as he realizes what's happening. I desperately swing at his face, but it doesn't even connect as he grabs my wrist, squeezing so tightly that I cry out in pain.

"Let me go!" I scream. "Nero!"

"Shut the fuck up!" Chase straddles me, his hands moving around my throat to choke me out. "Nobody's coming to save you."

He's wrong. I hear Nero yelling my name again, somewhere nearby, but I can't even draw a single breath. My lungs are screaming for air, and I struggle uselessly, desperate as I feel my body weaken, and my vision blurring at the edges.

Oh God, he's going to kill me.

I look up at Chase, pleading, but I see only a grim satisfaction in his eyes as he bears down, the pressure crushing my windpipe, and—

BANG.

Chase suddenly loosens his grip on my throat. His body crumples away, revealing Nero standing behind him, holding a gun in his hand.

"Lily!" He goes down on his knees beside me in the dirt, dropping the gun and cradling my face in both hands. "Lily? Talk to me?"

I wheeze for air. "I... I..."

"It's OK, baby," Nero vows, "Everything's going to be OK."

But I shake my head, eyes going wide with fear as I see Chase roll over and rear up again, face a mask of fury. "Behind!" I manage to blurt, pointing. Nero's gunshot only hit his shoulder; blood drips, but Chase doesn't seem to notice as he reaches down into his boot and pulls out a switchblade. The metal gleams in the sunlight—and the look in his eyes chills me to the bone.

Desperation can make a man do wild and dangerous things. But so can love.

Because Nero doesn't waver. As Chase lunges, Nero bobs to his feet and ducks away, then charges at Chase with a roar. I manage to roll clear, as the two men fight, down and dirty in the mud. It's a free-for-all, fists flying, the blade flashing. Nero slams his elbow into Chase's ribs, but then Chase attacks with a brutal headbutt that sends Nero reeling back.

Chase brandishes the knife, ready to move in for the kill.

"No!" I scream, scrabbling in the dirt to try and reach Nero's gun. But as Chase slashes madly, Nero ducks away. His expression is focused with fury as he moves with grace, that krav maga training in full evidence as he keeps out of the reach of the blade. Then, suddenly, Nero grabs Chase's knife hand and twists, wrenching it in a way that makes Chase howl in pain and drop the knife. Then Nero attacks, driving at Chase with a series of brutal, blunt blows to the face and neck, his fists the only weapons he needs.

"I trusted you!" he roars, pummeling Chase back, and then down onto the ground. "I fucking trusted you!"

Chase's face is bloody. He moans in pain.

"You forgot, I'm still a fucking Barretti," Nero swears, punching Chase so hard, I hear the crunch of bone. Once, twice, three times... "And Barrettis don't leave traitors alive."

Nero is merciless. And finally, Chase sags, unconscious. Nero grips his collar and lifts his fist again, ready to finish him.

"Nero!" I cry, and he pauses, as if remembering I'm here. "Nero, please!"

He drops Chase's unconscious body and is at my side in an instant. "Are you hurt?" he demands, fear etching his features. I nod. "Where?"

"Everywhere," I manage, wincing as he cradles me in his arms.

"I've got you, baby," he swears, holding me closer. "Nobody's ever going to hurt you again."

I breathe him in, feeling the warmth of his body, so safe and secure. "I was so close to losing you," I gulp. "And now, with Chase..."

"Shhh," Nero soothes me. "I promise, nothing will ever break us apart again. I'm never letting you go. *Never.*"

That's when the dam finally breaks. I explode into messy sobs, crying into his shirt as the emotion and terror of the past forty-eight hours hits me all at once. I feel like I've been run down by a truck, my whole body hurts. But when Nero holds me so gently, the terror fades.

He's here. He's holding me. And I'll never let him go again.

"I'm so sorry," he whispers, stroking my hair. "I love you so much. I'm sorry I tried to push you away. That woman, it was nothing, I—"

"I know," I interrupt him, wiping my eyes. "I love you too. "I couldn't go to Paris. I came back for you."

Nero manages a smile, cradling my cheek in his hand. "I should have known I couldn't tell you what to do," he says fondly. "Nobody can—"

I hear the faintest sound. A twig snapping. And then everything happens in slow-motion.

I look behind Nero, and see Chase on his feet again, bloody. Wild-eyed. Lunging at us with the knife in his hand.

I don't have time to think. I don't even have time to breathe. I snatch up Nero's gun from the dirt beside me, lift it, and fire, straight at him.

BANG. BANG. BANG.

The sound of the gunshots is deafening, echoing around the woods as Chase slows to a stagger, his face going slack.

Blood blooms from the middle of his chest, and then he falls to the ground.
    Dead.

Chapter 19

Lily

What happens next is a blur. Nero calls for help, and soon the woods are swarming with cops and paramedics. I'm led away to the back of an ambulance to be checked out, where I sit, numb and trembling while a sympathetic paramedic runs all my vital signs.

"I can't stop shaking," I whisper.

"It's the adrenaline." She smiles slightly, and I notice that she has a dimple in one cheek. It's strange, the things that I find myself focusing on right now. Everything just feels so surreal.

I killed Chase.

"What?" I ask, confused.

"The shaking," the woman explains. "It's from the adrenaline that floods your body when you're in danger. It what causes the fight or flight reaction. I'm guessing that you went with fight," she adds, glancing to the body bag being wheeled past

I swallow hard. "Not by choice."

She goes back to stitching up a cut in the back of my head, and I sit there, trying not to wince.

Nero strides over. He's been caught up talking to the cops, but he's been sure never to be far away from me.

"What's the verdict?" Nero demands.

"I'm fine," I insist.

"She'll be fine, eventually," the paramedic corrects me, finishing up. "But you need rest, and time to heal. No more cross-country runs or wrestling matches."

"That won't be a problem," Nero says immediately. "She's not getting out of bed for a month."

"At least buy me dinner first," I joke weakly. He doesn't laugh. Nero's looking at me with fierce protection in his eyes.

"So we can go?"

The woman nods. "I don't suppose you'll let me take a look at that cut," she says, nodding to the place where Chase's blade nicked Nero's arm.

"Nope. We're not spending another moment here. Come on."

He carefully helps me down from the ambulance and steers me over to his car. A cop meets us there. "Heading out?" he asks.

Nero nods. "You have my statement."

"Yes, but your wife..."

"Can talk to you back in the city." Nero gives him a cool glare. "She's been through enough today."

The cop pauses, but then gives a nod. "Fine. We'll take her statement later. It's a clear case of self-defense," he adds, reassuring me. "The kidnapping, attempted murder... I'm sorry you had to go through this."

I give a nod. "Thank you."

Nero puts me in the car, handling me like I'm made of glass. Then, finally, we're driving away, leaving the cabin in the rearview mirror.

I'm going home.

Ruthless Vow

When we arrive at the house, Nero insists on carrying me inside, scooping me up into his arms and taking me all the way up to our bedroom. I could walk, but I don't protest. It feels too good to be back in his arms.

"Are you hungry?" he asks, placing me gently on the end of the bed.

I nod. "I'd love something to eat. But first... I'm going to need to get out of these clothes," I say, glancing down at the muddy, bloodstained outfit I've been wearing for two days straight.

"Coming right up."

Nero draws a bath for me, and heads downstairs to the kitchen while it runs. He returns with a plate of cold pizza. "Sorry, this was all I had."

"Are you kidding?" I say, devouring the leftovers with delight. "I've never been so happy to see day-old pizza in my life before."

The bath fills, and Nero adds some of my favorite oils, too. Then he carefully helps strip my bloodstained clothing over my head. "Burn everything," I tell him, tossing the garments aside. He helps me into the tub, and I sink into the hot water with a sigh.

"Good?" he checks, testing the temperature.

"Amazing," I say. My body aches, but the water feels amazing. Nero soaps up a washcloth, and gently begins washing me, cleaning every inch of my skin in careful strokes, until I'm totally clean. Then he wraps me in a massive fluffy towel and guides me back to bed.

My heart melts. He's taking care of me in a way that no one ever has.

Nero sits me back down and fetches me a pair of pajamas. "I'll let you rest," he says quietly, turning to go. "I need to go start cleaning up Chase's mess."

"Wait," I stop him. "Are you coming back?"

He turns, and to my surprise, there's hesitation in his eyes. "That depends... If you want me to."

I stare. *Do I want...?*

"Of course I want you to," I exclaim, confused. "I told you, in the woods—"

"You were traumatized. You've been through a lot."

"No, we've been through a lot," I say strongly. "And we came out the other side. We have a second chance here, or maybe it's our third, or fourth, but either way, I don't want to miss out on this again." I tell him. "I don't want to have to miss *you*."

Nero's expression changes. He comes to me, holding my hand. "I'm so, so sorry," he swears again.

"You don't need to apologize for anything." I insist. "Well, except maybe trying to send me away, but I understand, you were only trying to protect me."

"I'd do anything to keep you safe, baby."

"I know."

His eyes burn into mine, and the depth of emotion there is astounding. He's held so much of it back from me, but now it's all laid bare for me to see. "I love you, Nero. You've always said I belong to you... Well, you belong to me too. Whatever the future holds, we're in this together."

"I love you so much." He kisses me softly, still taking care not to hurt my wounds.

Then he gets down on one knee, right there in front of me.

I gasp.

"I know you never got a real proposal," Nero says, with a bashful smile. "We got married for all the wrong reasons, but I want to do it right this time. I've always been in love with you, Lily, since the very first day I laid eyes on you. You're amazing. So strong and smart. You're tough as hell, and I can't get over the fact that you're mine. I've spent my life trying to be a man that deserves you, and I've failed a few times, but if you're willing to give me another shot, I'll come through for you. I want to be the husband you deserve. Will you be my wife?" he asks, gazing up at me. "For real, this time."

My answer chokes with a sob, but it was never in doubt. "Yes!"

This man has showed me the best of himself, and the worst, and I've loved him all the same. I'm meant to be with him—no matter what.

Nero rises to his feet and pulls me into a gentle hug, burying his face in my neck. I wrap my arms around him, as Nero kisses me. The embrace deepens, and I press closer, wanting him, but he pulls away.

"I don't want to hurt you," he whispers.

"You won't."

I stand, letting my towel fall to the floor before I lay back on the bed. Our bed.

Nero's eyes rove over me, and for a moment, I'm self-conscious about the marks and bruises. But there's nothing except reverence in his eyes.

He strips off his clothes, and joins me on the bed, his mouth covering mine again. Tenderness shimmers in the air as Nero softly runs his hands over my body, caressing me gently, leaving no part of me untouched. I hold him, reveling in the feel of him under my hands again. his strong body. The honed muscles that protected me, fought for me.

Bled for me.

Nero breaks our kiss, his lips making a path down my chest until he reaches my breasts, lavishing them with care until I'm moaning and gasping under his expert mouth. "Nero..." I whisper, already damp and aching at my core. "I just need you. Inside me. *Please...*"

"Anything you want, baby. I swear, I'll give you everything," Nero vows. He strokes me softly between my thighs, teasing my clit and dipping his fingers into my wetness until I'm more than ready for him.

I'm *begging*.

"Nero..."

"That's it, Princess." Nero lets out a groan as I find his cock and pump him hard in my hand. "It's all yours."

"And I'm *yours*," I whisper, gazing up at him. "All of me. I'm yours. *Take me*."

Nero's face is full of tenderness as he positions himself above me, and slowly thrusts inside. We both moan in pleasure at the feel of it, his cock filling me so perfectly.

"This pussy was made for me," Nero groans, pumping deeper, body tight with tension. "Fuck, baby, you feel so good."

"Yes," I moan, arching up. Loving the feel of him, claiming me, the way I need. But he's so gentle, I squirm, impatiently, chasing the rush that's still out of reach. "More," I plead, breathless. "Harder."

"Baby..." His eyes flash with concern.

I meet his gaze, and deliberately thrust my hips. "*Harder*," I demand again. "You know how I need it. Don't hold back."

"Fuck."

Nero pistons into me again, harder this time, and oh, it's perfect. So fucking perfect. "Yes!" I cry, matching him thrust for thrust. "Yes!"

"My filthy Princess," he groans, shifting angles, lifting my leg over his shoulder to bear down just right. "You need this cock all the way deep, don't you? Listen to you, demanding every last inch."

I cry out as he hits that sweet spot inside me, delirious with pleasure now. "Give it to me," I pant, writhing. I've never felt so free, so safe to show my soul. "Give your wife what she needs."

"Me," he growls, rutting into me faster. "I'm the only goddamn thing you'll ever need."

"Yes!" My voice rises as I feel the pleasure cresting. "Only you!"

"Gonna be a good girl for me?" Nero demands, groaning. "Going to come for your husband, show him just what this pussy can do?"

He finds my clit, and swipes it possessively, and I break apart with a scream, stardust bursting in my veins from the most epic orgasm of my life.

I'm still shaking with the force of my climax when I look down into his eyes. He's right there with me, shuddering his release, and more than that, I can see our future. It's written in his eyes, the promise of what's to come between us, the devotion and happiness.

Our future. Together.

And nothing can stand in our way.

Chapter 20

Nero

There's only one thing standing between us and the future Lily deserves. But I'm going to deal with it. Today.

I wake before Lily, which is a treat. I lie there beside her, listening to her breathe, simply enjoying the way her body feels, wrapped around me. She's burrowed against me in her sleep, head on my chest. It's as if she was trying to get as close to me as possible.

I can't believe I nearly lost her.

I resist the urge to hold her too tightly, just taking it all in. Chase's betrayal, and our final, bloody fight. It fills me with fury all over again, but I force myself to breathe deep. It's over now. The threat is gone, and I'm going to do whatever it takes to protect Lily from now on.

She's more precious to me than anything in the world.

She stirs, yawning. "Good morning," I whisper.

She looks up at me with a sleepy smile. "Morning."

Lily sits up in bed and stretches. Her beautiful naked body is bathed in sunlight coming in through the window, and even though the sight of the bruises marring her delicate skin make me want to kill Chase all over again—slowly—I know that they'll heal.

Nothing can break us now.

"How do you feel?" I ask.

"Fine," Lily replies. I give her a look. "OK, well, a bit bruised," she admits, rubbing her shoulder.

"The medic said you need rest."

She gave me a wicked smile. "You mean, lie in bed all day? Are you going to join me?"

I chuckle. "Tempting, but I have a meeting I can't miss. I'll be back later, though," I promise.

She pretends to pout, jutting out her bottom lip, and I lean forward to nip at it.

"I know how to make it up to you," I offer. "How about we take that trip to Paris... together? Let's have a real honeymoon."

"Really?" Lily lights up with a brilliant smile. "When?"

"I have a few things to wrap up here, and you need to take it easy," I remind her.

"Right." She grins. "How about next week? It'll give me time to plan everything we're going to see... Everything we're going to eat."

I smile, happy to see her so excited. "Whatever you want."

"Are you sure you can't stay?" she asks, leaning in to kiss me. Her breasts press temptingly against my chest, and I can feel myself getting hard just at the taste of her.

But I force myself to release her and get out of bed. "The things I need to do today, they can't wait," I say regretfully.

She watches me, looking concerned. "Dangerous things?"

I shake my head. "Things that will keep us safe forever," I tell her. "I made you a promise, and I can't relax until I see it through."

She nods, understanding in her gaze. "Good luck," she says softly. "I'll be waiting. Me... and Paris."

I hit the road, heading first out to Long Island to meet Igor Kovack on his home turf. He greets me warmly, offering me breakfast, and we set about finalizing the handover of Barretti territory and trading routes.

"No second thoughts?" he asks, after all the business terms have been settled.

"None," I say firmly, offering my hand to shake. I drove a hard bargain and got a cash deal that will more than take the sting off the new regime for my guys. It's a multi-million-dollar takeover we've just negotiated, but there are no lawyers, no settlement documents to sign that would never stand up in court.

Our word is our only bond.

Igor shakes firmly. "I wish you all the best in your new endeavors," he says, but I pause on the way to the door and look him dead in the eye.

"Don't for a minute take this as a sign of weakness or retreat," I tell him coldly. "If you overstep your boundaries, come after my family, or any Barretti men, in *any* way... All bets are off. I will burn your fucking castle to the ground."

Igor takes it well. "I wouldn't expect anything less." He nods. "Send my regards to your wife," he adds, showing me out. "I hear I have her to thank for keeping this agreement together and seeing off a costly war. And to that end..." he pauses.

"What?" I eye him warily.

"A little information I came by, a gesture of my goodwill, to help with your happy future." Igor pauses, a smirk on his face. "You might want to ask yourself why, exactly, that rat of yours tried to kill you."

Ruthless Vow

"Vance?" I blink. "The question's crossed my mind, believe me."

Igor smiles wider. "It never made much sense, did it? A loyal soldier of your father's, a man who always followed Barretti orders. Unless..." he pauses, with a knowing look. "Unless he was still following orders."

The blood drains from my face. "What do you know?" I demand, but he shakes his head.

"Whispers, rumors, that's all. But I'd be careful, if I were you."

I clench my jaw. "Thank you. And no offence, but I hope I never lay eyes on you again."

Igor's laughter follows me out. "Touché, Mr. Barretti. The feeling is mutual."

Still following orders...

I mull Igor's words all the way to the next stop on my list. I wish I could write it off as some kind of mind game, trying to fuck with me one last time, but Igor has no reason to pull that shit now. I just handed him everything he wanted. He's genuinely giving me a friendly warning.

The question is, what am I going to do about it?

I arrive at the prison, and take a moment there in the parking lot to get my shit together. Roman isn't expecting me today, but I figured the element of surprise would be best. The man is difficult enough to handle on a normal day, but when he hears my news, he's going to go ballistic.

I head inside, and wait in the visitation room for the guard to bring him in. This one has protective Plexiglass dividing us, and ugly orange chairs lining the table.

"You stupid little prick. What the fuck have you done?" he storms in, already furious.

I play it cool. "Hello to you too, Dad."

"Don't even call me that. You have no right," Roman roars. For the first time in a long time, the man's famous sense of control has shattered. He's practically foaming at the mouth. "I heard the deal you did with those Kovack fuckers! You've thrown it all away! Destroyed everything I built, for some goddamn whore—"

"Enough," I roar back, getting to my feet. "It's done."

"Like fuck it's done." Roman slams his fist against the Plexiglass.

"It's done," I repeat. "There's nothing you can do about it now."

Roman wheels away, pacing. "Should've throttled the bitch when I had the chance," he seethes. "Her and her rat father. Should've burned them in their sleep!"

I watch coolly. "Are you quite finished?" I ask.

He turns back. "You'd really do it, choose that cheap slut over your own family. Your own father?"

"Yes." I stare back at him, my father. This lion of a man, now caged and resentful. He raised me. He trained me. He taught me to put the Barretti organization above everything, to fight and bleed for it.

And I did. I soaked my soul in the blood of our enemies. I thought it was my destiny, that I was doomed to a life of cold, empty evil.

Until she showed me I could be something more.

"I choose Lily," I say it loudly, my voice ringing with conviction. "I choose her over you, a thousand times over. She's my wife."

Roman flinches like I've struck him, but he's not done yet. "You're pathetic," he sneers. "Cunt-struck and weak. She's made a mockery of you." He spits in my direction, the saliva hitting the Plexiglass divider. "You're no son of mine."

"And you're no father, either." I shoot back. "What father plots his own son's murder?"

Roman's eyes flash with surprise—and guilt.

"Yeah, I know about your plans with Vance," I continue, blood roaring in my ears at the confirmation of my darkest suspicions. "What did you figure, you'd have him rat on me, set me up with the Feds to get me out of the way? And then when that didn't work, you figured a car bomb would do the job instead."

"Do you blame me?" Roman sneers, "You're a fucking embarrassment. I'll do whatever it takes to protect the organization."

"And I'll do whatever it takes to protect my family," I reply. My anger gives way to ice-cold certainty.

There's only one path forward for me now. One last way to sever my ties with the past, the ties that hold me back.

I turn to the door.

"That's right, coward, run the fuck away!" Roman calls. "But I'll find you. I got people everywhere!"

"No." I turn back. "*I* have people. Barretti people. My men. And everything you have here in prison—your comfort, your protection—that all comes from my pocket. You signed it all over to me, remember?" I say. "Total control over all the assets, everything. The guards who bring you food, the cushy perks from the warden, those men keeping watch outside your cell, standing between you and all your enemies? They take their paychecks from *me*. But it's over now," I tell him. "As of today, you're on your own."

Roman pauses, and I can see the wheels turning in his brain. Putting the pieces together... And realizing just how many of the violent prisoners in the building have a vendetta against him.

"Now, wait a minute," he blurts. "Son, you can't—"

"You just said, I'm not your son," I remind him, walking to the door.

"Wait! They'll fucking tear me apart!" he cries after me.

I look over into my father's face for what I know is the last time. "So be it."

With those final words, I walk away, knowing that I'm leaving my toxic legacy behind for good.

Now, there's nothing standing in the way of my future with Lily.

I'm free.

Chapter 21

Lily

One week later...

I wake up in the most comfortable bed I've ever been in.
I stretch happily, a smile on my face. The suite at the Ritz is gorgeous, the height of luxury, with stunning antique furniture, a sitting area and a fireplace. We've been here three days, and I'm just about over the jet lag, but it's hard not to spend all day in bed when I'm in a palace like this.

And have my very own prince to keep me occupied.

"Nero?" I yawn, sitting up. I assume he's in the palatial bathroom, until I see a note left on the pillow beside me.

Getting breakfast, be back soon. X

I smile, getting out of the bed and pulling on the luxurious hotel robe. I hurry over to the massive widows, and pull back the drapes, letting out a sigh of excitement when I take in the perfect view of the Eiffel Tower. I don't even want to know what Nero splurged to buy us this amazing room, but it was worth it, every penny.

It never gets old.

"Was that a good sigh?" Nero's voice comes, and he enters the suite.

"The best. I can't get over this view," I say.

"Nothing like it." Nero's eyes rove hungrily over my body, and I giggle.

"I was talking about the view out there."

"Yeah. Sure. Whatever." He pulls me into his arms and claims my mouth in a sizzling kiss.

When we come up for air, I notice the white paper bag in his hand. I can already smell that something delicious is inside. "You didn't need to go out for food. I think the Ritz offers room service," I tease, and he smiles.

"The café two blocks down. I saw you eyeballing their croissants yesterday, so I decided they would make a good breakfast. They had fresh strawberries too. Redder than I've ever seen."

I smile, excited to try the pastries. All the food here is amazing, rich and decadent. Every meal is an event.

Including this one. Nero pulls back the curtains on the doors leading to the balcony, and I follow him out there. There's a small metal table and two chairs on the balcony, and Nero sets up our breakfast. He's brought coffee too, and I sit back, sipping the sweet brew. "This is perfect," I say happily.

My phone rings. "It's Teddy," I announce happily.

"Wait a sec," Nero reaches over and tugs my robe closed. "There, family friendly."

"Whoops!" I laugh, then accept my brother's video call.

"Want to see the most perfect croissant in the world?" I ask, taking a bite.

"More perfect than the pic you sent yesterday?" Teddy asks, grinning. "My message feed is nothing but food!"

"Because it's so good!" I retort. "Anyway, why are you up so late? Isn't it like three in the morning there?"

"I just got home from a party. I thought I'd check in. How's that husband of yours treating you?"

I glance over at Nero, who has a mouthful of croissant.

"Just fine, and he can hear you, FYI."

Teddy shrugs. "He gets it. We have an understanding."

"An understanding?" I raise an eyebrow.

"Yeah. He treats you right, and I don't kick his ass."

Laughter bubbles up in my throat. I can't help it.

"Don't worry about me, I can do the ass-kicking myself," I joke. "You just focus on school. Maybe do more studying than partying..."

"Fine," he says, letting out a long-suffering sigh, as if I'm the biggest nag in the world. "I'm going to hit the hay. I'll talk to you in a couple of days."

"Bye. I love you."

"Love you."

He ends the call, and I look over at Nero, who's already watching me. "You miss him, don't you?" he asks, and I nod.

"I'm glad he's doing so well with school, but I wish I could see him more."

"Then, we'll visit. Every month if you want."

"Amazing breakfast *and* the promise of frequent trips to Indiana?" I coo. "Are you trying to butter me up for something?"

"No way." He smirks and caresses my arm, "Although, now that you mention it..."

Desire flares in his eyes, and I stand. Walking into the suite, I leave the balcony doors open. Turning back to look at him over my shoulder, I untie my robe, and let it drop down to the floor.

He growls, stalking after me. He catches me halfway across the room, picks me up, and throws me on the bed.

"Nero!" I squeal, laughing. Then he's above me, pinning my wrists to the mattress with one hand as the other glides down my body, landing between my thighs.

"Already wet, baby?" he teases me, fingers nudging and probing.

"Always, for you," I reply, writhing against his grip. Loving how it feels to be at his mercy.

"So tight," he groans in appreciation. "Look at you, spreading those sweet thighs nice and ready for my cock."

"Are you going to keep me waiting?" I shoot back, with a challenging look. "Or are you going to fuck me?"

He chuckles. "Oh baby... Be careful what you wish for."

In an instant, he flips me over so I'm facedown in the sheets and lands a stinging spank on my ass. I make a noise of excitement, as Nero yanks down his pants, jerks my hips back, and fucks me from behind with a savage thrust.

"Yes!"

I scream into the pillows, feeling his thick length invade me, demanding.

"That's right, Princess," Nero grunts, slamming into me again. "I know how my baby wants it. And I'll fuck you up good, every goddamn day for the rest of your life. You'll like that, won't you?" he croons, twisting my hair in one hand, pulling my body up flush against his. The new angle is heaven, grinding up inside me so deep I sob in pleasure, arching back.

"Yes, yes."

"Yeah you will." Nero keeps up his punishing rhythm, driving me wild. "Because you live to please me. Just wake up in the morning, roll over, and open wide for my cock. You won't need panties, you'll only get them drenched, you can just stay naked and ready for me. Ready to serve my cock anytime I like..." His hand moves to my clit, playing with his palm splayed possessively over my lower abdomen. "Ready to get a baby in that belly."

Fuck, the thought is enough to make me come with a scream, my voice echoing in delight over the Paris rooftops.

And then Nero flips me over and does it all over again.

It's the perfect honeymoon.

* * *

As much as I love the wild, liberated feel of our lovemaking, it seems criminal to spend all day inside when the whole city is waiting to be discovered. Eventually, I drag Nero out of the hotel room to go sightseeing. The Louvre has always been at the top of my list, and it's just as amazing as I always imagined, with every kind of art that I'd ever heard of.

Sculpture, paintings, antiquities, even decorative arts... I spend a happy hour dragging Nero through the magnificent halls. But the paintings are what really impress me. "You know this museum has over seven thousand?" I chatter, eyes wide as I try to drink it all in.

"You mentioned it," Nero says with a grin.

" Raphael, Michelangelo, and da Vinci... Just seeing all those famous paintings in person is the experience of a lifetime."

"And there I was, thinking I gave you that this morning," he smirks, pulling me in and nipping at my neck.

I laugh. "You did. But look, it's amazing."

"You're amazing."

I blush, holding his hand as we walk through, looking at them all. Nero doesn't rush me, he's happy to listen to me talk a mile a minute about all my favorite artists, and even pulls the official docent over to talk when I can't find the answers in my guide.

We spend hours there, and I know I could stay even longer, but my stomach starts to rumble, and Nero reminds me that we have dinner reservations. So, I let him drag me out of the place, with promises from him that we'll return at least once more during our two-week stay in Paris.

We rented a car, and Nero drives us to dinner. I'm looking out the window, checking out the architecture of the buildings we pass and the people walking around on the streets.

I'm not paying much attention to where we're going, but when Nero pulls over in front of a designer boutique, I'm surprised. "What are we doing?"

He grins, a wicked glint in his eyes. "Well, if we're going to dinner, you'll need a new outfit."

"You brought me shopping?" my eyebrows shoot up. "You really are competing for 'best husband'."

"Come on." He shows me into the lavish store, where an attendant immediately helps pull gorgeous dresses from the displays, ushering me to the fitting room.

I step behind the curtain, and strip off to try the first one when the curtain draws back, and Nero quickly slips in with me.

"What are you doing?" I giggle, keeping my voice down.

He smirks. "I thought I'd lend a hand," he says. "Just in case you need help with a zipper or something."

"How thoughtful."

"You know me..." Nero backs me up against the wall. "I like this outfit," he says, trailing his hand along the curve of my breast.

"I'm in my underwear."

"Exactly."

I laugh and reach for the first dress. It's a silky slip with a plunging neckline and a pretty blue color, and I love it so much, the moment it settles over my body, I know I don't need to try anything else.

And from the heat in Nero's eyes, I can tell he agrees.

"This one," he says, breath turning ragged as he slides his hands over the silky fabric covering my ass.

"You think?" I pretend to ponder it, turning in a slow circle. "It's very sexy..."

"Like I said, this one." Nero moves to stand behind me, in front of the mirror. I sink back against him, watching his hands move over me in the reflective glass.

"See how it shows off every one of your delicious curves?" His breath is hot in my ear as

his hands curve over my breasts, teasing and slowly tugging at my nipples through the silk.

I stifle a gasp.

"Nero..." I whisper, as he keeps stroking.

"Look at you, baby. Look at the way you get all flushed when you're turned on."

His hands slide lower, massaging me through the dress. The feel is incredible, cool silk on my skin. Then he hitches up the fabric and slips his hand in my panties. I widen my stance, watching as his fingers delve, finding my clit and rubbing me in maddening strokes.

Voices suddenly come in the dressing room outside. Another customer, just on the other side of the curtain. "Nero," I gasp, trying to wriggle away, but he holds me tight. Pinning me against him as he curls one thick finger, and then another inside me. Our eyes meet in the mirror, and fuck, it's so hot.

I pant, pleasure rising.

"Shh, baby," he croons, fingers pulsing. "Keep that pretty mouth closed, so they don't know how close you are."

I bite back a moan.

"Mademoiselle?" the attendant calls. "Everything is alright?"

"I... Yes!" I blurt, my voice high-pitched. "Thank you!"

Nero bites down lightly on my shoulder. "Maybe I should pull back the curtain," he muses, his fingers working faster. Harder. "Let everyone see you like this, baby. Legs spread with your skirt up and my fingers buried in your juicy cunt."

He presses his palm down against my clit as his fingers pulse deep inside me and *fuck*, I come apart, Nero kissing me just in time to swallow my cry.

Pleasure wracks me, until he lets me go. "I can't believe we just did that," I gasp, blushing.

Nero grins, tugging my skirt back down and smoothing the dress. "Yes, you can. And our trip's just started. I plan to make you come in every designer dressing room in the city."

He winks, and saunters out of the dressing room, leaving me gasping.

When I finally draw back the curtain, I find the attendant tidying up—with a knowing look on her face. "I... Think we'll take the dress," I announce, my cheeks burning.

"Oui mademoiselle. I thought you might."

Dinner is delicious, on a candlelit terrace with four courses of incredible food and wine, but I barely notice a thing we're eating. I'm in a haze of joy, watching Nero across the table, holding his hand and trading kisses, like any other honeymooning couple.

The couple I thought we'd never have a chance to become.

"Let's take a walk," I suggest, when the meal is finally over. Nero smiles and takes my hand.

"Lead on," he says.

Ruthless Vow

We meander down to the River Seine, and stroll along the banks of moonlit water, passing other couples and people out late. His phone buzzes, and Nero pulls it out to check. "It's Avery," he says with a frown. "It's a weird time for her to call."

I sigh, bracing myself for some bad interruption, but instead, Nero declines the call and tucks his phone away. "It can wait," he says, giving me a smile. "Nothing is more important than my wife."

"Except that éclair you stole from me at dessert," I tease, and he chuckles.

"I'll buy you a whole bakery of éclairs to make it up to you, how does that sound?"

"It sounds like we have our plan for what to do tomorrow."

We walk a little way further, the breeze warm. It really has been the perfect few days. "You think this will last?" I whisper, voicing the fear still lingering in the back of my mind.

Nero doesn't have to ask what I mean, we're already so in tune.

"I can't promise it will always be like this," he says, looking over. "We're only human. We'll fight, and bicker, and have hard times, as well as the good. But I promise, I'll always face those hard times beside you."

I stop walking and pull him down for a kiss. "I love you so much."

"I love you too," Nero vows. "We're forever, you and me," he whispers, and I smile.

I like the sound of that.

Avery

"*This is Nero. Leave a message.*"

BEEP.

I slowly lower the phone, feeling a weird sense of relief that he didn't pick up. I don't have to say the words out loud just yet, the truth that's just ripped my life apart.

Miles is dead. Nothing will ever be the same again.

"Avery?" One of Nero's guys hangs back, by the doorway. Looking freaked out now he's heard the news. "Do you know...? His family, I mean. Should someone...?"

"I know his mother," I reply dully. "I'll let her know."

"OK. Cool. Uh... I'm sorry," he offers. "I know you guys were close."

Close.

I stare at the wall. That's one way of putting it. I've been in love with Miles for years now, I dreamed that one day we would be together, but we never shared so much as a single kiss.

Now we never will.

I look down, at the crumpled note in my hand. The only thing Miles left me, the only explanation for his unthinkable act. The words blur behind my tears, but I already know them by heart. Branded on my soul.

I fucked up. I got in too deep with Sebastian's card game, I tried covering from the accounts, I thought I could win it back again, but I failed. I let you down. I'm sorry.

The card game. Sebastian Wolfe's high-stakes poker match, I've heard people talk about it—and the man who rules it with an iron fist. He's a billionaire hedge fund owner, adored and feared across the globe. Untouchable.

Or so he thinks.

But Sebastian Wolfe will pay. I'm going to destroy him, no matter what it takes.

Or I'll die trying.

TO BE CONTINUED...
Avery and Sebastian's epic story of vengeance and love gets started in PRICELESS KISS, available now!

PRICELESS KISS
Priceless: Book One

Vengeance is priceless… Discover the spicy, thrilling new saga from USA Today bestselling author Roxy Sloane!

Sebastian Wolfe is a billionaire hedge fund owner, adored and feared across the globe.

Untouchable. Or so he thinks.

I was prepared to give everything I have to make him pay for his crimes.

My innocence. My body.

My life.

But it turns out, to have my revenge, he'll demand the one thing I can never let him take:

My *heart*.

Roxy Sloane is a USA Today bestselling author, with over 2 million books sold world-wide. She loves writing page-turning spicy romance full of captivatingly alpha heroes, sensual passion, and a sprinkle of glamor. She lives in Los Angeles, and enjoys shocking whoever looks at her laptop screen when she writes in local coffee shops.

* * *

To get free books, news and more sign up to my VIP list!

www.roxysloane.com
roxy@roxysloane.com

Printed in Great Britain
by Amazon